MW01383321

Dear Ali,
Hope you & ...
Would love to see you
Good bless + take care!

Joe Stephens

Harsh Prey

A Shalan Adventure

by

Joe Stephens

HARSH PREY

Dedicated to all my students and friends who encouraged me to
finish this book.

HARSH PREY

The world is grown so bad
That wrens make prey where eagles dare not perch.

Richard III

First, I want to thank my students who encouraged me to pick up the pen (in the electronic sense) again and get this book finished. I imagine it was so they could quit hearing about how I was a frustrated novelist and start at least hearing different complaints, like how no agent has the good sense to represent me. But seriously, so many of you told me that I could do it and that I should. I can honestly say that I would never have finished this book without you guys.

I also want to thank Sandy Tritt, who edited the beginning of this book and taught me the ins and outs of self-editing. With your help, I took a bloated, self-important blob of a book and turned it into a sleek, smooth, quick read that I think people will actually enjoy. Thank you so much!

Next, I want to thank Officer Chris Morehead, the Prevention Resource Officer at my school and a veritable fount of knowledge about police procedures. I was amazed at what I didn't know and at how patient you were, Chris, in answering all my sometimes stupidly simple questions. I deeply appreciate you, not only for your help with this book, but also for all that you do to maintain a sense of sanity at PHS.

Next, I want to thank the late, great Robert B. Parker, my writing hero. The day I picked up *The Godwulf Manuscript,* my literary life changed. I can say without question that Harry and Dee Shalan would never have existed if not for you. I wish I could have told you that in person, but I hope you're somewhere that you can hear it now.

Finally, I want to thank my family and friends for all of your support and encouragement throughout this process. So many kind words that I can't even count them all. You have no idea how much it means to me

I know I said finally in the last paragraph, but over and above all of the folks I've mentioned is God. Throughout the writing, editing, and publishing of this book, as well as the rough personal times I've been experiencing, I've felt the warm and comforting presence of God more acutely than ever before in my life. No success would have any meaning if I didn't know I was saved by the blood of Christ, so to him I give the glory.

Chapter 1

The blast of a train horn started me from a sound sleep. I looked around the room, shaking my head to clear it. It was daylight and the sun shone brightly through the window of my third-floor apartment. Something seemed odd about that, but, at first, I couldn't focus enough to figure what. Slowly, I realized the room was flooded by sunshine because the blinds had fallen from their assigned position once again.

As my head cleared, I became more aware of the window, which had been open during the night and high winds had apparently blown the blinds from the loose wall bracket. *She would have made me fix that.* I stepped to the window to attempt repairs. Winds had apparently been accompanied by rain—a great deal of rain, judging from the splat sound my foot made and the abundant liquid squishing up from the carpet between my bare toes.

Great. I stepped through the living room to the bathroom and grabbed some towels. Nice start to my day. Scared from a sound sleep an hour-and-a-half before I had to get up, the Ohio River running through my bedroom and a large cockroach trying to carry away my soap.

I grabbed a formerly white tennis shoe from the floor and sent the roach to insect heaven. Or hell. Who knew? I was getting quite good at killing bugs. Too bad it was never this easy to take a human life. It was the hardest part of being a private eye. Even killing people who are more repulsive than a roach is difficult.

I rummaged around the kitchen junk drawer until I found a sticky note and pen and wrote a reminder to talk to Mr. Williams—again—about the bug problem. Like the broken blind bracket, this wasn't a problem when she was here. Our place, a high-end attic conversion in what was once a single family in the historic district of Parkersburg, was immaculate not so long ago. I stuck the note to the television screen where I wouldn't miss it—but it immediately fell off. Sticky notes don't adhere well to dust. This made me look around the room. Newspapers were strewn around the floor from wall to wall. It looked as if a printing press had gone wild. Dirty dishes and pizza boxes were piled on the table, precariously waiting for a nudge or breeze to topple them onto the paper-covered floor. This had once been such a nice place. Before.

"How long has it been?" I asked aloud, though the roaches and I were the only parties present. As I stepped into the shower, I calculated that she had left three months ago. In that time, I'd received only two short emails assuring me she was fine and that I shouldn't try to find her. I was ninety-nine percent certain where she was, but I respected her wishes, even though it was quite possibly the hardest thing I'd ever done.

I stepped out of the shower and looked in the mirror. A shade taller than six feet, I was, in her words, absolutely delicious. I didn't see it. I was already developing my father's high forehead, though I kept my sandy hair cropped closely enough it was hard to tell. Years of long-distance running, weights, and martial arts training had kept my frame lean and muscular and held the family jowls at bay. A jagged scar above my left eye was partially masked by my eyebrow. It was her favorite place to kiss. I was saved from the abyss by the sound of the land line phone ringing in the dining room. *Not many people call that number anymore.* I reached the phone on the fourth ring, picked it up while drying the left side of my head with a towel and held it to my freshly scrubbed ear. "Shalan."

The silence on the line was mitigated only by the faint hum of the wires. "Shalan," I practically shouted.

The silence continued. I held the receiver to my ear long enough to know that whoever was not talking to me was quite possibly spending money to do it long distance, though that is harder to know nowadays, due to digital technology. I nearly slammed down the phone.

"Harry?" a soft, feminine voice said.

A chill swept over me in spite of the warmth of the air, and my heart felt funny in my chest, almost like its tail was wagging. I wasn't sure I could speak. I swallowed hard and rubbed my tongue along the roof of my mouth in a vain attempt to find some moisture. "Dee?" It came out strained. She would think I was mad or disappointed or I hated her.

"So. How are you?"

"That depends. Are you calling from your cell phone downstairs?"

"I wish. I'm still far away, at least physically. I just needed to hear your voice."

"Well, you've heard it," I said in a way that came out snide. I wasn't sure how I meant to say it, but snide sure wasn't it.

"Yes. I guess I have." She sounded sad.

I was blowing it. "Listen, Dee, I'm excited to hear your voice too. Believe me, I need it. I never stopped needing it. You just kind of caught me off guard. I didn't think I'd ever hear from you again."

"Oh no, Mister Man, you aren't getting rid of me that easily. I just needed some time to sort things out."

"Well. Um. " I rubbed my unshaven jaw. "Are they?"

"Are who what?"

"Sorted out? Are things sorted out?"

Another pause. My heart, which felt funny before, came to a stop. The air left the room as I waited for the reply that I both longed for and dreaded.

"Almost, but not quite yet."

I feared I would suffocate. I needed oxygen. And Dee.

"It won't be long. I do know that I miss you—a lot. And I need you. Badly."

Oxygen filled my lungs and my heart resumed. I wandered into the kitchen. Before I could gather my thoughts to reply, a crashing sound came from downstairs. Based on the initial boom, followed by wood snapping and splintering, someone, probably large, had just destroyed my front door, which, due to the narrowness of the attic layout, was at the foot of a short stairwell. I dropped the phone, grabbed the pistol I had stashed behind the microwave, flipped the dining table onto its side, and dove behind it.

Deanna shouted my name over and over, but I couldn't answer her. I kicked a chair out from under my feet as the back door glass shattered. Barring a weird coincidence, there was more than one bad guy. The back door, which led out onto a small fire escape-sized porch, was around the corner in a small alcove, so I couldn't see it from where I was. I slid out from behind the table to the stove at my right, and leaned against it, bracing myself to fire at the thug coming up the stairs, but all that came up was the sound of the intruder struggling to free himself from the door that had apparently wedged itself into the narrow stairwell. Deciding I had time, I slid right again, past the refrigerator to the narrow brick column beside it that had once served as a chimney before the house was converted to central heat. The guy on the back porch fumbled for the lock handle. I'm not sure why he didn't just kick it in, but his decision would cost him. He didn't realize the lock was an oddball that required a key from both sides. Because of this, I kept the key hanging on a nail in the kitchen for just such a situation. I'd never seen such a lock before and haven't since, but it literally saved my life. I dove around the corner, just barely missing the kitchen sink on my left, and slammed into the doors of the recessed cabinets. The porch guy saw me dart by and fired wildly in my general direction, blowing a grapefruit-sized hole in my bathroom door. Big gun or crappy door? Both. I quietly opened the cabinet door to my left, reached in, and pulled out a yellow metal bowl. Inching up to the corner, just out of sight of the back door, I tossed the bowl over my left shoulder in what I hoped was the intruder's direction. Thud. Grunt. It had hit its mark. I rolled over, came up on one knee facing the door and fired three times at his chest.

The shooter, thrown off balance by the force of the bullets, staggered backward to the porch railing. He dropped his gun and reached a beefy hand up to touch the life pumping out of his chest. The vest of his three-piece suit blackened. He stared at me with a look of disbelief. I turned away and swallowed down the gorge that filled my throat.

His legs gave way and he rolled down the steep wooden steps to the second floor landing. I heard the snap of the rotting floor boards giving way under the newly-dead weight.

I didn't have time to mourn, though, because the second intruder had fought his way past the front door and was now at the top of the stairs. The short, chubby man wielded a nickel-plated .357 magnum as he leaned against the wall, preparing to fire. The gun glinted in the sun showing through the skylight above the dining room. I fired first, diving back to the protection of the small sink area. I fired again, conscious of the fact that I had just one round left and no way to reload.

I expended my last round to hold him off and made for the back door, but stopped short when I was reminded of what had impeded the entrance of the dead guy. The key that was not in the door had saved me, and now it was going to kill me. The key was there on its nail, but could I take it down, dance barefoot around shards of broken glass to the door, and get it unlocked in less time than it took him to take aim from ten feet and pull the trigger? I'm good, but I'm not from Krypton. I turned slowly, raising my hands, the barrel of the .357 pointed at my chest.

"Okay." The man in the blue suit sneered through thick pink lips. That one word revealed he was foreign. "I finally have you, Shalan. My associate was indecisive, but that is of no consequence." German. It was a thick German accent. That, combined with the long, jagged scar beneath his lower lip triggered my memory. Rutger Stultz. He and his brother had moved to the States after the Berlin Wall fell and had set up shop in Chicago. It was unusual to see a gunsel that expensive in tiny little Parkersburg.

He paused, savoring the moment—always a dumb idea. In the instant before he could pull the trigger, a metallic click filled the room and a shiny blue-gray shotgun barrel poked him in the side of the head. He was so shocked that his shot veered wide of the mark, killing nothing but the freezer door. I never liked that fridge anyway. Stultz's eyes rolled back as the air seemed to leave him and, as he deflated onto the floor, a bear of a man stepped around the corner behind him.

Bull Shannon really did look like a shaved bear. He was as tall as I, but outweighed me a good forty pounds. And he wasn't fat. I knew that if we ever fought hand-to-hand and he managed to get hold of me, the fight would be over quickly. I also knew he would never be able to lay a hand on me. Huge he had—not so much on the quick. Luckily, it wasn't an issue, since I trusted him with my life.

"Bull, sweetie," I said with a mock look of horror, "he's turning purple. Maybe you should take your boot off his throat."

"Oh!" He jumped back. "Sorry. I was too busy admiring your birthday suit."

I looked down and realized for the first time in a while that I was, as they say, *au naturel*. Stepping into the bathroom to retrieve a towel, I tried to wrap my mind around what had just happened. I had just gotten out of the shower when the phone had ru—DEE!

The phone was nowhere in sight, so I dove behind the table, throwing flotsam and jetsam in every direction until I finally found it and picked it up. Where the ear piece had been was now a mess of bent plastic and wires. They shot my phone. For reasons I can't explain, I put it to my ear anyway, apparently hoping it would miraculously work despite the missing parts.

It didn't.

Crap.

Chapter 2

I managed to get dressed in a pair of light gray gym shorts, a *News and Sentinel* Half Marathon shirt, which was the cleanest one I could find, and white ankle socks, before the police arrived. The first uniform on the scene was a kid I knew. Nice enough, but he had a problem with sarcasm, a problem I shared. He looked around for a few seconds before he spoke. "Good grief, Shalan, I knew things were tough, but you this hard up? Is it even legal to run a garbage dump in the city limits?"

"Ahaha, very good. Shut up." It wasn't my best line, but it had been a long day already. "In case your people haven't already noticed, there's a stiff one out back. Be careful—the wood is old and he hit hard."

As Bull and I spent the next hour describing the events of the morning to one cop after another, I changed out of my slightly odoriferous gym clothes and into work clothes, which consisted of well-worn jeans, a light blue polo, ankle socks and old running shoes. The parade of cops ended with Lieutenant Otis Campbell. I'd known the good lieutenant for most of my life. We'd graduated high school together, then I went to college while he went into the police academy. We had taken widely divergent paths but both ended up being crimebusters. He knew me—and respected me as much as I respected him. Of course, we would never say that to each other, but it was there.

"So you have no idea who hired Stultz?" Campbell asked for approximately the eleventy billionth time.

"No idea whatever. He said, 'I finally have you,' like it was personal. I've made him mad a few times, but I can't imagine his being mad enough to have a hit put on me, let alone come all the way from Chicago to do it himself." I rubbed away a bruised bump that had risen on my wrist. Must've smashed it while dancing with the gunmen. "There had to be money in it. A good bit of money, based on the firepower he came with."

"Firepower you disposed of rather quickly."

"It was my turf. They hadn't done their homework."

"Still pretty impressive gun play, though it was definitely lucky Bull showed up when he did, or Stultz would have perforated you."

I thought about that as I tried Dee's cell phone for about the fifteenth time. Straight to voicemail again. I hadn't heard from her since my phone was shot to death. Exactly what I needed—she struggling to deal with what I do and finally makes a big enough breakthrough to call me, and I go and try to get killed as she listens on the phone. The seething ache in my chest was back again. It was like a branding iron was being pressed into my heart.

Campbell was on his cell when I hung up; he nodded and grunted something unintelligible, then snapped the phone shut. "Stultz is awake, though he's still pretty loopy. Skull's cracked. Keeps jabbering about Chicago and Berlin and somebody named Tuttle."

"Tuttle?" My head whipped around. "Jonathan Tuttle?"

"I don't know. Who's Jonathan Tuttle?"

I was already halfway down the stairs before I figure he caught on to the fact that I was leaving. I hadn't heard them say where Stultz had been taken, but there was only one hospital in town, so it seemed a logical guess. I hit the bottom step of my building running; I gripped my car keys and hit the keyless entry when I was close enough. I had to get to the hospital and talk to

Stultz as fast as possible. It was surely a coincidence. Surely. Chicago's a huge city. How many Tuttles are there? And I didn't even know if this Tuttle was named Jonathan. But coincidences usually don't turn out to be coincidences in my line of work. Stultz was from Chicago. Johnny Tuttle was from Chicago. He and his family were the only people I knew in Chicago, my only friends there—well, except for Stultz, and I was pretty sure he didn't count. He wasn't somebody you'd bring up in conversation. Oh, you're from Chicago? I know a cold-blooded murderer from there named Stultz. You know him?

Chapter 3

Stultz wasn't all there when I got to his room, but he knew who I was. He shot me three times in the chest the instant I walked through the door. Luckily, he was only packing a finger, so the damage was minimal. After he stowed his weapon, he pulled out an imaginary phone and made a call. "Tell Johnny it's done."

I grabbed him by the front of his gown and shook him. "Johnny who, you piece of crap, Johnny who?"

"Leave him alone!" A nurse squared her shoulders and glared at me.

I dropped the jerk. He just looked through me, his eyes glazed and detached. He seemed to try for a few seconds to focus on my face, but it didn't work—the fog was just too heavy. I could see that trying to beat anything out of him, as fun as that sounded, would do no good.

I was on my way out the door hitting my speed dial as Campbell got there. He did a one-eighty and followed me. The phone rang ten, eleven, twelve times before I finally gave up and put it away.

"Still can't get in touch with Dee?" he asked.

"I haven't tried since the apartment. I'm trying to find Johnny Tuttle."

"Okay, I'll ask again—who is Johnny Tuttle?"

I tried to keep from sighing, but I did anyway. I glanced down at my feet. "My mentor."

"Your mentor? In what?"

I looked at him, trying to describe what I had never really put into words. Eventually, all I could come up with was one word. "Life."

He looked at me, puzzled. I thought about it for a few seconds as we waited on the elevator. The doors opened and we entered.

"He was a professor at my college. He taught literature, and it was a small school, so I had him for like six classes before I graduated. I was chronically homesick, so he and his wife kind of took me in. I was at their house for dinner three, four nights a week. I even babysat their kids."

If it weren't a violation of the guy code, I would have also told Otis that Johnny and I stayed close after I graduated and moved to Louisville. I especially missed my dad. I was the youngest of our family by several years and my dad was basically my best friend. Johnny kind of filled that hole when I was away from home. He didn't just teach me about great literature and how to appreciate it— he, along with my real dad, taught me everything that's important. He taught me about honor, ethics, chivalry—the importance of doing the right thing and what it means to be a good man.

Campbell grunted. I ignored him. I lowered my voice and spoke to my knees. "If there's any good in me, it's because of him."

"So what's he got to do with this guy?"

"Hopefully, nothing. Probably a coincidence. It's just that they're both from Chicago."

"Do you know how many Tuttles there are in a city the size of Chicago? Sixty-one, according to whitepages dot com." He never forgot anything, but why he'd know this was beyond me.

"Stultz thought he killed me and then pulled out an imaginary phone to report my death. He called someone named Johnny."

Chapter 4

I was supposed to meet with a client—a friend, actually, who had asked me to spy on her husband. I don't normally work for friends like that. It's just too much of an emotional minefield. I liked this woman and wouldn't mind keeping her as a friend, so telling her that her husband was schtupping another woman—or man for that matter—it is the twenty-first century, after all—was not exactly conducive to that. People tend to attach blame to the person who tells them bad news. It's not right, but it's still true.

Unfortunately, that was the news I had to share with this friend, Rebecca Howe. I would tell her as little as possible and answer any questions she might ask, hoping she didn't want to see the pictures. I've found that, despite the fact they already suspect they are being cheated on, people tend not to believe you when you tell them. A defense mechanism, I guess.

I had fifteen minutes to get to my appointment after I left Stultz and his delirium at the hospital. Clouds were gathering as I left the front door of the hospital, suggesting more rain. In the few minutes it took me to get to my car and out of the parking garage, the suggestion morphed into outright insistence. A tall, gray-green thunderhead loomed directly ahead of me as I turned left onto Murdoch Avenue. It covered the sun, forcing me to turn on the headlights on my dark green 2005 Mustang by the time I passed the Grand Central Mall. I had agreed to meet my friend at Jackson Park, another mile or two up the highway, where she worked as a manager of the municipal swimming pool. As I turned on my blinker and turned right, the rain came in sheets. There was no pitter patter of a few warning drops. It was just not raining and then suddenly it seemed I was driving underwater. The angry wind buffeted the car as if some unseen power was trying to stop me from driving up 34th Street toward the park. Maybe I wasn't supposed to tell this woman what I'd found out. Maybe I think too much.

The universe must have realized its efforts were for naught, for the wind abated as I pulled into the parking lot of the community building across the street from the pool about five minutes ahead of schedule. The rain continued to roar, albeit somewhat less vociferously than before, on the convertible top and windshield of my car. I left the engine running and the wipers on. After a minute, my friend's car, a red, older model Mercury Lynx, pulled up beside mine. I killed the engine, picked up the envelope of pictures I hoped she wouldn't want to see from the seat beside me, and reached into the backseat for my umbrella. I know, I know. Umbrellas don't exactly scream "hardboiled thug," but I'd forgotten my trench coat and the heavens were still wide open. At least it wasn't the girly purple one Deanna had gotten me years ago that I had carried reluctantly out of respect for her until it mercifully succumbed to a sudden gust of wind. I was appropriately morose when I reported the loss to Dee, but hurried to replace it with the more masculine black number I now sported.

Becca leaned over to unlock her door as I circled her car. She had small children, so I wasn't surprised to see her pitching toys and fast food bags into the backseat as I opened the door. I closed the umbrella as I got in, taking a good soaking in the process. There's just no good way to close an umbrella while trying to get into a car. You work so hard to stay out of the rain and then have to get your arms and legs wet trying to close the stupid thing.

Rebecca Howe was twenty-eight years old, but looked at least fifteen years older at the moment. Her shoulder length, wavy tresses were pulled back tight in a ponytail, which was being held in place with a clover green scrunchie. Her lips, normally full and voluptuous, simply seemed puffy in the middle and pinched in around the edges, drawn down into what had become a chronic frown.

"Hi, Becca. How are you?" I asked, realizing as I said it that it was a moronic question.

She was normally a hugger, but her arms were crossed tightly across her chest, as if she were trying to hold shut a hole where her heart had been. She looked straight ahead and down at her feet. I knew her to be a bit vain about her feet, usually keeping them perfectly smooth and pedicured; the toenail polish, always coordinated with her clothing, was never less than meticulously maintained. This day, the nails were too long, the polish badly chipped.

She didn't say anything, so I waited a minute, but nothing changed. Eventually, I got too uncomfortable with the silence and put my hand on her shoulder. She blanched back as if my touch had scalded her.

"Becca, I'm so sorry." I withdrew my hand with a jerk. I didn't know what else to say, so I didn't say anything. I realized I was spinning the envelope of pictures, so I stopped.

The sudden change caught her eye, and she put out her hand to ask for the envelope.

"You don't want to see these," I said.

"Who is she?" Her voice was gravelly. She kept her hand out, palm side up.

I knew she would know the woman. I should've left the pictures in the car. She may not have asked had I not been fidgeting with them. Too late, idiot. I handed them over.

She slowly lifted the flap on the envelope and slid out the pictures. The first was all she needed to see. Her forlorn face became pallid, then blotches of red started over her nose and spread across her sculptured cheeks, growing darker and darker until her face turned purple. I could see her devastation turning to rage as her hands trembled.

"Diane Chambers?" she screamed. "His secretary! I can't believe my life has become such a cliché! My husband is screwing his secretary!"

I'm sorry didn't seem sufficient, so I sat silently, not knowing what to do next. She decided for me after what seemed like a day or so, but was probably more like a minute, which is about how long it took her to look through all the pictures. She bit her lip that was now thin and tight, and put the photos back in the envelope. "What do I owe you?"

"Oh, no. No. You don't—"

"You did your job; it's not your fault my husband is a philandering ass who can't keep his wick dry."

The only other time I'd heard that phrase was in *The Right Stuff* when John Glenn told Gordon Cooper that he needed to keep his wick dry or he'd make the Mercury astronauts look bad. As I thought about that, I realized yet again that I'm much too easily distracted.

"No, seriously, Becca, I'm just glad you aren't mad at me. Please, if I can help a friend with my skills, I'm happy to do it. I'm just sorry it turned out this way."

She thought about that a few seconds and then slowly nodded. "Harry, thank you. You're a good friend." She leaned over and hugged me.

I was surprised at that, but squeezed her back. "What are you going to do?" I asked after the brief embrace ended.

"I don't know. For now, I guess Woody and I will stay with my parents while I get my head on straight. At least Woody's out of school for the summer."

She and Sam were from Louisville, where Dee and I had lived for eighteen months. Ironically, Sam was a seminary student too, but at a different school. They were our downstairs neighbors in a three-story house that had been converted into three apartments. It was by bizarre coincidence they moved to Parkersburg and we took up our friendship again.

"Well, again, I'm sorry this has happened and that I'm the one who had to break the news."

"I needed to know. Needed to confirm that I wasn't just being paranoid."

She stared off into the distance as the rain, which I just realized had nearly stopped, started to gain force again. The anger was being replaced by despair again. Her shoulders hunched over and she squeezed her arms together, protecting the hole in her chest once more. "What could I have done differently?"

"It's not your fault your husband is a philandering ass who can't keep his wick dry. You're a great wife and a great person. This is on him."

I could have told her about my doubts regarding Sam over the years, but it served no purpose at the moment. Maybe another time. Right now it would sound like *I told you so.*

She smiled wanly and leaned over to kiss my cheek. "Thank you. I love you, Harry. You and Dee have been such great friends." She leaned back and tossed her strawberry blond ponytail behind a shoulder. Her dark eyes seared into me and her voice grew quiet, almost to a whisper. "I hope you pick me and not Sam."

When a couple breaks up, their friends try to figure a way to stay amicable with both, but it rarely works. They end up, intentionally or not, picking one or the other with whom to stay friends. "Of course, Becca. You'll always be our friend, and we'll always be here for you. Never doubt that."

I knew it would be a struggle for her, though. People she knew as part of a couple would not be comfortable with her, at least until she started dating and could again do couple things. People think first of the big, emotionally draining things when it comes to divorce, but it's the little day-to-day discomforts, like having to be a third wheel on outings, that wear on people after the initial trauma has eased.

She thanked me again and looked at her watch. The forecast called for this storm to pass by late morning, so she needed to get to work opening the pool. I had to go home and see about fixing my broken home—physically, at least. It made me sad to think things may never be fixed between Dee and me.

As I drove toward home on Grand Central, the rain stopped and the sun broke through the clouds. A double rainbow formed over the hills in the distance. I, and all the humanity surrounding me, slowed. For just a few seconds, strangers were joined in shared awe.

Too bad those kinds of things don't happen more often.

Chapter 5

I parked in front of our apartment, my mind a tangle of thoughts. How could I help Becca through this? Was John Tuttle really trying to kill me and, if so, why? I hadn't seen him in years and our relationship had never been other than one of respect, admiration, and love. How could that have changed? Overriding all other worries, though, was Dee. How did hearing what happened this morning affect her? Did this push her over the edge, convincing her there was no hope for us to ever be happy together? Could she ever learn to deal with the fear that I may not come home someday? Could I change for her? Give up this work that, in so many ways, defines me? If I did give it up, would I still be the man she fell in love with?

My head swam hard against this maelstrom of questions, so hard that I was at the opening where my front door was supposed to be before I realized sounds emanated from inside the apartment. I froze. I knew I was preoccupied, but I was sure all the cop cars were gone when I parked. I stuck my head around the corner. Domestic sounds—sounds of water running, dishes being scraped, cabinet doors opening and closing—came from within. Maybe Bull and his wife Roz cleaning up? Maybe the landlord? Maybe a waiting killer who got bored and decided to do some cleaning? Maybe— no. I wouldn't hope that. I couldn't. I was too afraid.

A four-legged, furry, fifty-pound torpedo thumped into my chest. As I tumbled to the floor against the wall in the stairwell, a wet tongue covered my face with licks so numerous they threatened to drown me. "Hey, Eddie! I know, I'm glad to see you too, but you gotta get off me. I can't breathe!"

Eddie, our fawn-colored Boxer, eventually calmed enough to let me up, but continued to lick my hand, my neck, my leg— anything that was in range of his freakishly long tongue. He was just barely past puppy stage and was, to say the least, energetic, despite what we had been told by our vet about dogs calming down after being neutered. Finally, when I was upright, he jumped into my arms and laid his head on my shoulder like a baby being burped. It was our thing.

I carried Eddie into the apartment. The most beautiful sight I had ever seen—or ever would see—waited for me. I pulled Eddie, who had calmed down, away from me and placed him on the loveseat, which, I wouldn't notice until later, was now no longer covered with laundry and newspapers. He circled a few times and curled up, letting out a sigh of contentment. Mommy and Daddy together again.

Chapter 6

As it pretty much always did when I first came into her presence, the world around Dee got fuzzy, making her stand out in relief. Her fiery auburn hair was slightly longer and she had lost about five pounds, which made her already gloriously healthy breasts appear even larger, but other than that, my beautiful bride was exactly as she was the last time I'd seen her—the last time I was fully alive.

She fell into my arms and it was like we'd never been apart. From the first time I'd ever hugged her, it was clear that our bodies and souls were made for each other, like we were two pieces that made a whole. As I held her, I kissed her on the forehead on my spot, just at the hairline on the right side of her face. She inhaled deeply through her nose and held it for a few seconds.

"God, I missed your smell," she finally said. "I took some of your cologne with me, but it's just not the same when it's not on your throat."

"Remember when you gave me this cologne for the first time?" I settled my chin on top of her head, inhaling the intoxicating scent of her luxuriant mane. The aroma was a mixture of her natural scent and an obscenely expensive shampoo that was the only kind she had ever used in all the years I had known her. Like she was with my cologne, I had smelled her hair care products on other women, but they never approached the dizzyingly lust-inducing bouquet that emanated from my Dee.

"Remember? A woman doesn't forget the night her man proposes to her—especially when it's in a White Castle."

"Well, to be fair," I retorted, "that wasn't the intended location."

We had told the story to friends and family what seemed like a thousand times. Dee and I had met six months before the White Castle incident, and had felt an immediate and powerful attraction. We started dating the same night and were basically inseparable from then on. For our first Christmas together, I made reservations at Six-Ten Magnolia, our favorite place in Louisville. It was way too pricey for everyday dates, but this was obviously a huge occasion, though Dee was not aware of just how big. Unfortunately, my car at the time was somewhat less muscular, not to mention dependable, than Ellie, my current ride. It simply did not like cold weather, which we had that night, for the first time of the season. It wouldn't start and I didn't have the money for both cab and dinner, so I had to swallow my pride and call Dee for a ride. By the time she got to my apartment and we made our way across town to the restaurant, we had missed our reservation. Six-Ten Magnolia is only open for public dining a few days a week and was, as usual, slammed, so they couldn't get us another table for a week. So we decided to go to our other favorite Louisville eatery—White Castle.

As we sat in the restaurant eating our sliders, she could tell something was up. I'm normally a clown, especially at the Castle, where we both knew everyone who worked and ate there. But this night, I ate quietly as I stared into her chocolate eyes, which normally danced with mischief, though they shone with concern that something was wrong as she watched me fidget through my meal. "Are you okay, honey? Please don't worry about dinner. You know I don't care about that. I'm happy anywhere as long as I'm with you."

I smiled at her and knew I couldn't wait another week to ask, so I decided to plow on, the somewhat-less-than-romantic location be damned.

"Dee, I know we haven't been together for that long, but I pretty much knew the minute I heard your angelic voice that I wanted to be with you for the rest of my life. I always told people that I hoped you were beautiful because when I heard you singing, I knew I was going to marry you someday."

She put her dainty hand over her mouth. Her perfectly manicured nails were painted a pale shade of pink. Her eyes started to glisten with tears as I slid out of my seat and onto one knee on the floor beside her, reaching into my pocket for the box.

"Babydoll," I said, opening the box to reveal the ring, "I've never known or been known by anyone like you before, and I know that will never change. The air has more oxygen when I'm with you and the sun shines more brilliantly. I want never to stop feeling that. I love you more than I ever would have guessed I was capable of loving anyone. You make me want to be the hero you think I am. Will you please marry me?"

She was so shaken with sobs that she couldn't form the word, so she just kept nodding as she held out her left hand for me to put the ring on. Before I could get up, she dropped to her knees in front of me and crushed me with a hug. I honestly couldn't say how long we stayed there, but I held her, whispering I-love-yous in her ear until her crying subsided, and when we finally came to our senses and started to rise, it was to the enthusiastic cheers of all the employees and patrons of the restaurant. She laughed and covered her face for a moment, but then had to pull her hand away to look adoringly at the diamond on her ring finger. She had kissed me tenderly as we walked out the door and to the car.

I was jolted back to the present by Eddie, who had been patient as long as he could be and now pushed his nose between the two of us. We broke our embrace and turned our attention to our baby.

Chapter 7

We worked on the house as I told Dee about the day's events, including what the cops and crime scene techs hadn't already told her, and about Rebecca and Sam. We didn't talk about the fact that she was back, what it meant, or whether it was permanent. I wasn't sure I wanted to know the last part.

I covered the holes in the refrigerator door with duct tape, then turned and faced Dee. "I have to go to Chicago."

"Chicago?" Her eyes stopped sparkling. "Why?"

"I need to find out if Johnny is involved in this—and if so, why."

"He couldn't be, Harry. I mean, really. You know the guy. He's not going to send some hit man after you."

"I know." I sighed deeply, all the stress of the day expelling with my breath. "I know. But somebody put a hit on me, and whoever it was had something to do with Johnny Tuttle and Chicago. I have to go there and find out why."

She studied my face as though she could crawl under my skin and read my mind. Sometimes, she could. Finally, she sucked in a lungful of oxygen. "You're right. We've got to get to the bottom of this. Otherwise, they may try again."

We've. She said *we've.* I couldn't hold back my smile. "You gonna come with me?"

Again, she was quiet, just looking at me. "I just get here and you have to leave." She looked away, taking a big chunk of my heart with her. "I want to be with you, but I'm sure Becca needs a shoulder—a female one. I can commiserate with her about how bad our men have been to us."

I wasn't sure if she was joking, so I let it go.

"I'll keep trying to call Johnny, and I'm sure Otis is already reaching out to the local leos up there and seeing if they will make some inquiries. This whole thing may be a giant misunderstanding, and maybe I won't have to go." I waited for her to turn her eyes back in my direction. "Who knows—maybe there's another Johnny Tuttle. A bizarro one."

I fully believed I'd be making the trip, but I wasn't going to say that. I'd learned over the years to trust my gut, and my gut was telling me that something was going on, and Johnny Tuttle—my Johnny Tuttle—was somehow involved. I wasn't prepared to conclude he was trying to have me killed because that simply made no sense whatsoever, but the fact that our apartment was riddled with bullet holes forced me to consider it.

We worked in silence for a while, her on cleaning and me on repairing and throwing away. Mr. Williams would take care of the structural damage, giving me the bill, which I would submit to my insurance. Despite my masterful duct tape plugs, the fridge was a goner, so we'd have to get a new one. Luckily, there was nothing edible in it that would go bad. We would need to do something about that too.

After the cleaning and repairing went as far as it could, we got Eddie onto his leash—somewhat akin to leashing a big hairy Super Ball—and took him for a walk around our neighborhood. The rain had ushered in a cold front, so, while the air was still damp from the storm, the temperature had become much more clement than usual for this time of year. It also seemed to make everything instantly greener and lusher. Ours was a generally well-tended neighborhood of historic homes. Some, like the one where we lived, had not been as well maintained, but many were showplaces, with long front yards festooned with ornate landscaping. The flowers and shrubs were in their full glory after a second storm in two days, which had broken a brief dry spell. Augmenting the visual beauty was the almost cloyingly perfumed air, thanks to Bea Taylor's prize-winning rose garden.

As we walked, Dee took my hand in hers, raised it to her lips and kissed it gently. Something clicked deep in my soul. She was home, so I was home too, for the first time in three months.

"I thought you were dead," she said.

I kind of let it hang for a bit, mostly because I had no idea how to respond. Eventually, words—clumsy, useless words—came. "I'm not." Beautiful, Shalan. And you used to be on the speech team.

She ignored my moronic reply. "I wasn't sure I could go on if you were gone. I didn't even stop to tell Mom and Dad where I was going. I didn't pack, I didn't do anything except get Eddie and his leash and run for the car. I had to know, I had to be in your presence. I knew then that my need for you and my connection to you is more vital to my survival than anything else in the world. And part of being in your life is accepting that you are, more than anyone I know, what you do."

"A big chunk of what I am is you, Dee. I am not me without you."

"I know, but you are also not you without doing what you do. It's what attracted me to you in the first place, and it's what draws me inexorably in now. I can't live without you and I can't live with myself asking you not to be a detective, a hero. It's like asking Superman to turn in his cape. You help the helpless, support the weak. You do heroic things because you are, with every fiber of your being, a hero."

"I just try to help," I replied sheepishly. I never knew how to respond when she talked like this. I hated and loved hearing every word she said, not because I loved the thought of being a hero. What meant so much to me was that the person who made my heart beat thought it about me.

"It's that beautiful, self-deprecating manner that I know is not put on, that makes you all the more irresistible. I'm pretty sure I would simply cease to be if you died, but I'm equally sure that I cease to be, in any way that is meaningful or attractive to me, if I cease to be with you."

"So what you're saying is you love me." I smiled and bumped my hip into hers as I waved at Ike and Corabeth Godsey, who were enjoying the cool air and brilliant sunshine from the shade of their broad front porch. Ike smiled from his oak swing, which was suspended by chains from the porch ceiling, and raised a glass of lemonade as if to propose a toast to us. In response, Eddie barked and leapt high into the air. He pretty much loved everybody, but he especially loved Ike and Corabeth, not in small part because she gave him bites of her homemade bread every time we stopped by on walks.

"My love for you was never in question, Mr. Studly." She skipped over a chunk of broken sidewalk. "The only question was whether the fear of losing you was too much to live with. Now I know the fear is just part of the price I pay." She squeezed my hand. "And it's more than worth the price."

We stopped. Eddie stood with his front paws against the trunk of Ralph Parker's hickory tree staring with utmost concentration at what I assumed to be a squirrel only he could see. Squirrels were Eddie's mortal enemies.

I turned to face Dee and pulled her into my arms. "I love you, Dee. More than anyone has ever loved anyone before."

Our lips met and the whole world went away. No Eddie, no neighbors mowing lawns, no kids shouting and running—just her and me. At least until a car horn pierced our bubble of passion and simply would not stop. I guess we should've picked somewhere other than Old Man Parker's driveway to declare our eternal love for each other. We smiled and waved, unembarrassed, and re-commenced strolling down the walk. As we reached the corner, Otis Campbell's city-issued Crown Victoria pulled up beside us.

Chapter 8

With an impish grin on his face, Campbell got out and walked quickly to Dee, enfolding her in his arms for a long hug, followed by a kiss on the forehead. Dee responded by wrapping her arms around her old friend and locking her left hand around her right wrist and squeezing with all her might. It was their thing. She gave him one last hard squeeze, eliciting a grunt from him and a crunch from his back.

"Ah, Dee, I'm so glad you're back. Next time you two do this, you stay and make that big buffoon leave. The city is much more pleasant with you here."

"I missed you too, sweetie." She smiled up at him as she stepped back to put her arm around the small of my back while I draped my arm over her bare shoulder. Just touching her skin, any quantity of her skin, was like an electric shock. I squeezed her slightly to my side in a way that was probably subconsciously territorial.

Otis and Dee had dated in high school, but not seriously—not for her, at least. Though we never discussed it, I knew, just in a way that guys understand each other, that Otis had always carried a torch for her, but also knew he would never act on that feeling. He would never have an affair with any married woman, but his respect for me added another level of prohibition.

"I'm sure you would come here just for the opportunity to try to steal m'lady from me, but I bet you have news," I said.

The smile disappeared as he reached into his jacket pocket for his phone. He tapped the touch screen a few times to access the information he needed. He held it far from his face trying to read the tiny text before remembering his reading glasses, which were, as always, perched atop his head. He slid the black half-frames onto the bridge of his nose and nodded slightly as he examined the now legible lettering.

"Jonathan Adams Tuttle, born September seventeenth, nineteen-fifty-three, at Winchester Medical Center in Winchester, Virginia. Is that your man?"

"I don't know the hospital," I replied, "but I know that's his birthday and that he's from Virginia. His parents were Dylan and Olivia Tuttle."

"There you go—Dylan and Olivia Tuttle," he repeated. "I have spent the last couple hours following his trail, which was pretty much normal right up until about six months ago, when he and his wife, Lilith Moon Tuttle, basically disappeared. No bodies have shown up who are likely to be either of them. Their phones are all disconnected and the house is being maintained by lawn care and housekeeping services, but no one has heard from them. Friend of mine on the Chicago PD ran out there and asked around. There were people mowing the grass and watering plants, but none of them had ever seen the Tuttles. They get paid by and receive instructions from the company they work for, Second City Econogreen Lawn Care and Landscaping Company. My friend said he would follow up with the company's headquarters, which is actually in Joliet, to see if they know anything about Tuttle, but I haven't heard back from him about it yet."

Otis swatted at a bumblebee interested in his cell, then refreshed his screen. "They still have checking, savings, and a money market account at Bank of America, as well as Visa, MasterCard, American Express, and various store credit cards, all in both their names. Five years back, over a period of a couple months, he withdrew all the money in the bank accounts, maxed out the credit cards, and took out a second mortgage on their house. We couldn't find any change in his reported income, yet within months, his credit cards were paid in full, both mortgages were paid off over a matter of just a few months, and he now has a healthy balance in both his checking and savings accounts."

I frowned. "Any clue as to where the money came from?"

"Nope. Detectives haven't had a chance to track down any of their friends, though my buddy went to a few houses in the neighborhood and asked around. Nobody has seen the Tuttles for years, despite their house being regularly maintained. He's a friendly guy who always checks in with his neighbors; say hello, have a barbecue now and then. One guy said he had seen him one day about two years ago and waved, but Tuttle didn't wave back, which was apparently unusual. Next day he was gone and hasn't been seen since. Oh, and they apparently now get their mail through a PO Box. My friend checked and it's picked up regularly."

I listened with growing alarm to Otis' report, amazed at how quickly he had gathered so much information, but scared at what the facts implied. At best, they had disappeared of their own accord, for reasons that were not readily apparent. Worse was the possibility that he had been forced to disappear; the worst prospect was, and my stomach got heavy even thinking it, he and was dead.

Chapter 9

Dee and I discussed it at length for the rest of the day, going back and forth several times, and finally reached a compromise. I would drive to Chicago, leaving the next morning, and Dee would spend the day with Becca, and then fly to Chicago the following day. That would give me an evening and part of the next day to get some checking around done before she arrived. I wasn't comfortable with her being with me if things went badly, but I was even less comfortable with her being home and vulnerable to attack while I was some five hundred miles away. Mostly, I was uncomfortable with the idea of being away from her now that we were a happy couple again. But I needed to work and she needed to be there for our friend, so we met in the middle.

That evening, after going to the store for a few items we would need before we left, we got takeout from the Chinese place near our house and ate at the picnic table in the back yard.

"My flight takes off from Wood County Airport at 9:36 a.m. on Tuesday," she said, teasing a shrimp from the cardboard carton with chopsticks, one of many things she was so much better at than I.

"I have a two-hour layover in Cleveland, and the flight from Cleveland to Chicago will be about an hour and a half, so, with the time change, I'll land at O'Hare at twelve-thirty. Will you pick me up or should I take a cab to the hotel?"

This was a rhetorical question. All husbands worth their salt know that. The idea that I would not be there to pick her up was ludicrous to both of us, but she asked anyway.

"What gate?" I asked.

"E-fourteen in terminal two, but my baggage claim is in terminal one; you can just meet me there."

She leaned over and put her head against my left shoulder. I kissed her on top of the head and popped the last of my dinner in my mouth. She was less than half finished with hers. I could chase down, kill, skin, cook, and eat a moose in the time it took her to eat a pint of shrimp, vegetables, and noodles. But she wasn't really interested in eating anymore anyway. Nor was I. She slipped the bright green flip-flop from between the toes of her perfectly pedicured right foot and ran her soft sole up the front of my left leg, an action which caused an immediate reaction from both my soul and my body. The feeling of her dainty foot, combined with the sight of her beautifully straight toes, whose nails were painted my favorite shade—deep purple—were like throwing gasoline on what, up to then, had been a smoldering fire. There was a tall hedge around the backyard and I knew the Williamses would be gone for another two hours, so I boldly picked her up from her seat beside me and put her on my lap, burying my face in her porcelain-skinned neck.

"Oh my!" Her eyes widened in mock surprise. "Is that a gun in your pocket, or did you really miss me?"

"Both!" I growled as I nibbled on her throat. I worked my way up her chin until our lips met and it was too late to try to get inside. Our need was too great for modesty to overcome. A flood of pent-up yearning for each other rushed out of us and, for the first time since we were randy newlyweds at the Jungle Drive-In, we made love outside.

Several minutes later, we headed inside to continue things in a more conventional way. Just as I buckled my belt, Mr. and Mrs. Williams came through the back gate, about an hour and a half earlier than planned. The movie they wanted to see was sold out.

Luckily for all involved, they stopped for ice cream instead of driving straight home. Mrs. Williams had an odd smile on her face, and I suspected she knew what we'd been up to, but it may have been my imagination. Still wrapped up in each other, we bid a hasty goodnight to our landlord and lady and ran up the backstairs to our apartment, giggling like children, Eddie romping enthusiastically behind us.

Chapter 10

Being a morning person, I was up by 5:00 a.m. I usually set the coffee on automatic so it's ready when I get up, but we were somewhat busy the night before, so that was the first order of business. Once the coffee was ready to brew, I was out the door, down the steps, and into the street for a three-mile run. I hadn't run for a few days and had let my training fall off a little bit since competing in a local 10k race a few months before. But the events of the previous day had re-invigorated me.

As I ran down my street, turned right, then crossed Park Avenue into City Park, I processed the events of the last twenty-four hours. Had it been just one day? So much had transpired. When I got up yesterday, I wasn't sure I would ever see Dee again; yet this morning, I woke up beside her and it looked like we were better than ever. Granted, on the less positive side, some goons tried to murder me, but hey, they clearly failed, so there's that. Maybe worse than the attempted murder was the unthinkable accusation that it was at the behest of the person who was almost like a second dad to me. At the very least, Johnny was in trouble and needed help—the kind of help I was good at providing. And if he was trying to have me hit, there had to be some tragic reason. A psychotic break, a physiological ailment that drastically altered his personality, some situation in which he had to choose between his family and me—my mind swirled, grasping for explanations. I knew there would be no answers, though, until I found my mentor.

After two laps, I stopped at the entrance to the park and stretched out my right hamstring, which never seemed to loosen up, then took one more lap before cutting through the entrance and out onto Park Avenue. I must've been too absorbed in thought, though, for as I stepped into the street, I noticed for the first time, a dark, fast-moving blur just a short distance up the street to my left. I backed quickly onto the sidewalk as a car seemed to materialize from nowhere. Its lights were on when I looked at it, but I was certain they hadn't been just a few seconds before. The car accelerated and jumped the curb, threatening to smash me into the stone base of the park entrance archway. I dove behind the base with no time to spare as the car careened off it with a crunch and scrape, rattling the wrought iron sign that spanned the entryway hard enough that I wasn't convinced it would stay upright. The base buckled slightly but held. Rather than stop, though, the heavily damaged car gunned its engine, throwing mud and grass with its spinning front wheels before getting purchase on the asphalt again and surging back onto Park Avenue. The car, an older model Chevrolet or Pontiac—it was still too dark to know exactly what color it was—continued to accelerate. As it pulled away, the driver turned his head just long enough that I could see he was male with dark hair and a moustache, but he was gone before I could see anything more. Without realizing I was doing it, I was on my feet and sprinting in pursuit. I hoped the driver had pushed his speed too much and wouldn't make the turn at the end of Park Avenue where it dead ends into Twenty-Third Street at Mt. Olivet Cemetery. My hopes were dashed, though, as he somehow managed to negotiate the left, using every inch of road as well as several feet of grass and the chain link fence bordering the cemetery. By the time I got to the corner, the car had cleared a slight rise and was out of sight. Having just run three miles, I was spent and knew I had no chance of catching up on foot even if I had been fresh, so I stood staring up the hill for a minute as I caught my breath, and then jogged toward home.

Park Avenue is a long, straight street with no parking allowed on the park side, and it was still dark enough out that I should've noticed the headlights coming. I felt certain he had been driving without them. I initially assumed it was simply a drunk, but it took a pretty good driver to make that turn at such a speed, especially considering the damage he'd done to the right front fender and tire. My gut said this was no accident, so I stayed extra alert all the way home in case they guy circled back, but I made it home without incident.

Finished with my run, showered, and feeling bulletproof once again, I made scrambled eggs and added some shredded pepper jack cheese. I filled and folded two whole wheat burritos with the egg and cheese mixture, ladled on several spoons of homemade black bean and corn salsa, and then refilled my coffee mug. Before sitting down with the paper, which I had picked up from the stoop on my way in from running, I wandered around for a few minutes trying to find my reading glasses. They were on the TV this time. Finally, I settled down at the kitchen table and ate as I caught up on the previous day's news.

I was on the front page, below the fold. It was the usual news with no real information—big and splashy, like every non-natural death in a small town, but with practically no specifics. Someone killed. Identity unknown. Police had no comment other than to say it appeared to be a case of self-defense. There was a fuzzy picture of the back steps with police tape across them.

"Harry Shalan of Parkersburg, who is believed to have pulled the trigger in the fatal shooting, was not available for comment at press time." Not available at press time? I was available at press time. Why would they say that? Oh, maybe it had to do with my phone getting murdered. I reminded myself to add that to the note I had written for Dee.

Breakfast eaten, dishes put in the dishwasher, and my teeth brushed, I went over my luggage one last time. Satisfied that everything was in order, I walked quietly into the bedroom, trying not to wake Eddie, who always slept at the foot of our bed. The not-waking-Eddie part was no problem—he had taken after his mommy rather than me and was not a morning person. I looked down at Dee's glorious, angelic face and pushed aside a lock of her auburn hair before kissing her on the forehead. She stirred, though I didn't think she was awake until I started to walk away, only to be pulled by a belt loop with surprising force onto the bed.

"Don't even think of leaving without a proper goodbye, Mister Man!" She pounced on me like a tiger on a fresh kill.

"I need...to get out of...town and to...Chicago as soon as possible...sweetie," I protested between kisses. It's hard to talk, or think, for that matter, when a gorgeous creature is trying with great zeal to molest you.

"Chicago can wait." She nibbled my ear. My weak spot.

"It's nine hours." My conviction wavered. Resistance was futile. Heck, I didn't even want to resist, but I really did have to get to Chicago.

"Ellie's fast—you'll make up time."

Ellie was fast, that was true. Besides, what kind of fool would I be to turn down the sexiest, most beautiful woman on the planet? That she chose me has never ceased to amaze me. I gave in and kissed her back, lifting my old t-shirt—her favorite night wear— over her head as she started working the buttons of my shirt. Even though we had made love just the night before, the thrill of seeing her naked still made my heart race. How lucky could one guy be?

HARSH PREY

That morning, quite lucky.

Chapter 11

Satisfied in every way, I finally hit the road again just after 9:00 a.m., though I didn't get far before I picked up a tail. A really sloppy one, at that. He was sitting in his car a short way up the block from our house. I may not have noticed if he hadn't started his engine as soon as he saw me approaching. He pulled out from a few car lengths behind me as soon as I left the house and he was immediately near enough most of the time that I could actually make out his features, which, frankly, made me kind of wish he wasn't so close. He had a long, narrow face that also managed to look doughy. His nose was long and hooked nearly over his mouth, which was covered by a poorly kept moustache of a color that roughly matched the dull gray of his hair, though most of his head was the same color as his pasty face. He was the victim of a truly unfortunate comb-over that was made all the more regrettable by his driving with the windows down on his car, a dark brown 1986 Chevy Cavalier with some pretty extensive damage to the right front quarter panel. I was relatively sure I knew where that damage came from.

He was either a complete moron or was trying to follow someone for the very first time. When he nearly rear-ended me at a red light, I concluded it was likely all of the above. So this guy blew at both vehicular homicide and tailing people. Whoever hired him should demand their money back.

As the light turned green, I floored it, turning left from the right-hand lane, narrowly missing two cars, one in each direction. The driver of the second car informed me that I was number one and I could see him mouthing something that I couldn't quite make out, but it might have been Brother Tucker, who is, we all know, the patron saint of illegal left turns. My tail, caught off guard, tried to follow me, but only succeeded in hopelessly snarling traffic in all directions. He was now the new number one.

I sped up and turned right on Emerson Avenue, then pulled off the road, through a Wendy's drive-through, and parked in the lot of a bowling alley. I was about to put in a call to Otis Campbell when the Cavalier came rolling into the lot. Unbelievable! How did this muttonhead find me? As my dad used to say, he couldn't pour piss out of a boot if the directions were printed on the sole. But when he parked five spaces away and got out, I realized he hadn't found me at all. He didn't even know I was there. It was just pure dumb luck that he'd happened to pull into that lot. I called Otis and got out of my car quietly. He was animatedly talking into a cell phone when I walked quietly up behind him and put the barrel of my gun against the back of his head. Being as brave as he was smart, he immediately dropped the phone and put his hands above his head.

"You are, without question, the worst bad guy ever. First you miss running over me, then you come closer to hitting me when you're trying to tail me. It really burns my bacon to see somebody take so little pride in his work. I mean, the only way you could be worse at this would be to have a sign on the front of your car that says, 'I'm following you!'"

Beak Nose turned his head a little and shrugged helplessly. "Ich spreche kein Englisch." Just for good measure, he said it about a hundred more times. He wouldn't stop, not even to breathe, which gave me hope that he might eventually pass out. I knew it meant "I speak no English," but I couldn't get him to shut his schnitzel hole long enough to say it. When the cops got there, he proudly told them, "Ich spreche kein Englisch, Ich spreche kein Englisch, Ich spreche kein Englisch."

"You have all of Germany after you, Harry?" Otis asked as he stepped out of his car. "It's good to see you're now a multicultural pain in the ass."

"It's important to broaden one's horizons."

"I thought you were leaving for Chicago early this morning. Why are you still here?"

"Something came up."

Otis gave me a knowing look, but let the comment pass. I told him about the attempt to run me down earlier that morning and the comically bad attempt to follow me. As the uniforms searched the Cavalier, Beak Nose continued to serenade us with his one line chorus.

"Oh, will you stifle it already?" Otis yelled. He shook his head. "Hogan, cuff him and take him downtown for booking. Let them listen to him for a while. And find Sergeant Schultz when you get there. I think he speaks some German. Maybe he can find this jackwagon's mute button."

I grabbed Otis's arm and pulled him away from the others. "Listen, Otis, I need your help. These dimwits aren't very effective at bad guy stuff, but they seem to be pretty persistent. Would you mind babysitting Dee until she flies out tomorrow?"

"Sure. I'm on until 6:00 p.m., but I can assign a uniform to stay with her until then."

"No, you needn't do that. I'll call Bull and have him go over and check in on her until then. She's going to be visiting with a friend in a couple hours anyway. Maybe you could put a car on her while she's out?"

Otis nodded, shot me with a finger pistol, and pulled his phone from his pocket as he walked back to his car.

I called Bull and arranged a visit from him and Roz, then called Dee and explained the situation, about which she was less than happy; however, she finally agreed not to lose the cops when she saw them. She was more than happy to have Otis over for the night, though. Glad I'm not the jealous type.

Chapter 12

By the time I pulled out of town, it was ten a.m. The weather was perfect, so I had the top down and Michael Bublé blaring on the stereo. Under other circumstances, it would have been a fun trip.

I had hoped to make it to Indiana before stopping for lunch, but the events of the morning made that impossible, even with the granola bar and apple I brought with me, so I settled for making it to the far side of Columbus. I pushed it nearly to Dayton, when I decided it was either stop or give in and start gnawing on my arm, so I pulled off where I knew that there was a Penn Station restaurant nearby and ordered a turkey sub, which I managed to eat with a minimum of damage to my shirt, and made good time, stopping only once more for a bathroom break at a rest area on I-65, just a little north of Indianapolis. I had programmed the address of my hotel into my GPS and followed the directions without any trouble. Even though I'd been in Chicago a few times, it was reassuring to have that voice telling me when to turn.

It was late when I finally got there, so I walked down the block to a Chipotle restaurant, where I had chips and salsa and a vegetarian salad. Because it was so healthy, I decided to reward myself when I got back to the room by getting a bag of M&Ms out of the vending machine. Actually, I got two. One pack never seems to be enough. I ate one in the elevator on the way up to my room and polished off the second as I fired up my laptop. After checking my email—nothing worth answering—I called Dee on Skype.

"Hello, lover," she said, "I miss you already."

"I would ask what you're wearing, but Skype kind of ruins that."

"I can cover up my webcam and lie if you want," she said with a wicked grin.

"I'd rather see your glorious face, but maybe later."

"It doesn't matter anyway," she said, "because I'm spending the night at Becca's. There are kids everywhere."

We talked about nothing in particular for a while before I was just too tired to keep my head up.

"I'll meet you at the end baggage claim. Dee.

"I can't wait, my darling," she replied heavily. Her eyelids drooped over her normally bright eyes.

"I love you, Dee. Forever."

"Love you too, Harry. Try to get some sleep. Goodnight, sweet prince."

I couldn't hold my smile. "And flights of angels sing thee to thy rest."

Chapter 13

After a better than expected night's sleep, I was up by 6:00 a.m. and across the street to the fitness club with which the hotel had an agreement. I did thirty minutes on the elliptical, then bypassed the machines and went for the free weights. It was an upper body day, so I did chest flyes, military press, French press, biceps curls, and balance ball crunches. I generally do three sets of each exercise, but I was kind of pressed for time, so I did only two sets this session. I hadn't pushed myself like I usually do, but it was the best I could do for the moment, so I was happy with it.

The club had a smoothie bar, so I breakfasted on a strawberry banana smoothie with an extra shot of whey protein and as large a coffee as they would sell me, which wasn't nearly large enough, but then, no coffee is large enough for me. Caffeine—my drug of choice.

I was showered and getting dressed when my cell rang. It was Otis, with news—or, in actuality, with an announcement that he really had no news. The lawn and landscaping company had no information. Their contract to maintain Tuttle's property had been initiated via email and all the contracts were sent to a PO Box, which was no longer assigned to anyone, and returned via fax, which turned out to have been sent from a local office supply store. All instructions were sent via email. The address was a Gmail account, but the information given when it was set up turned out to be bogus and all the emails were sent from various locations, from public libraries to restaurants. No two emails had come from the same IP address. Nobody at the post office, supply store, library, or any of the restaurants remembered anything that was helpful, and the last email had been sent too long ago for there to be any security footage. Again, I was amazed at how fast Otis and his colleagues worked and simultaneously at how little information that work had yielded.

That left me with two avenues of investigation: Northwestern and Tuttle's neighbors. I only had time for one before I needed to get to the airport to pick up Dee and I knew she had always wanted to see Northwestern, so I drove to Johnny's neighborhood to begin the tedious task of knocking on every door I had time to and asking the same questions over and over again in the usually vain hope that somebody somewhere knew something that somehow might prove helpful sometime.

I programmed Johnny's address, which was in Evergreen Park, into my GPS and then headed out of the hotel's parking garage. Tammy, as Dee and I had started calling the narrator on our GPS, announced in her prim British accent that it would take me approximately 40 minutes, something which I always took as a challenge. I got there in 37 minutes.

"Still undefeated Tammy. You can't beat me."

She simply told me that I had arrived, but I could hear the sense of defeat in her voice. Tuttle's house was at the end of a cul-de-sac with a raised railroad track at the back of the property. It was a modest house, though well maintained, which made sense considering the maintenance was being contracted out.

I planned to canvass the neighbors, but it seemed logical to check out Johnny's house first. It was a 1.5 story house. It had powder grey vinyl siding with black decorative shutters. A two-stall attached garage was on the right side of the house at the end of a flat 15-foot concrete drive that had seen better days. The work and materials had been shoddy when it was poured and the surface was sloughing off in places and grass was growing through cracks almost everywhere. Someone who had a coolant leak parked on the far right side pretty regularly, but not too recently, based on the age and size of the stain. Centered above the double-wide garage door, which matched the shutters in color (though, based on the lack of fade, it had been replaced at least once since the house was built), was a basketball backboard with a shredded hole where the rim had once been. One too many thunder dunks. A sidewalk, apparently poured by someone other than whoever perpetrated the drive, led straight from the left side of the driveway and made a ninety-degree right turn after about eight feet and went another six feet or so to the front porch, a shallow number that ran from the end of the garage to the far left side of the front of the house. There were two forest green plastic Adirondack chairs with a round outdoor grade end table made of frosted pebbled glass in a chipped, rusting white aluminum frame. One of the legs was missing its protective foot and had been replaced with duct tape, I guess to guard against damaging the green indoor-outdoor carpet. I never understood why bright green was such a popular color for this ubiquitous eyesore. Someone told me once that it was supposed to simulate grass, but that didn't make sense to me. First of all, it's not even close to the color or texture of grass and second; it's never used in place of grass, except maybe on goofy golf courses. It would have been somewhat less offensive to the sensibilities had it been coordinated with the house colors. But, as usual, I digress.

The black, six-panel front door was behind a standard aluminum storm door, the top glass panel of which was slid down to allow air flow through the screen. Not surprisingly the storm door was unlocked. Somewhat surprisingly, so was the front door. Not just unlocked, but slightly ajar and as I stood there, I realized two things. One, my gun was in my hand despite my not remembering having taken it out of its holster. Two, the smell of putrefaction was growing stronger as I leaned closer to the narrow opening in the door.

My stomach turned over and I swallowed back bile at the thought of what may be causing the unmistakable stench of rotting death that was undoubtedly emanating from inside this house that was supposed to have been empty since the last time the Tuttles had been seen six months ago. I quietly closed the storm door, being careful not to let it click too loudly when it latched, and slid to the left the few feet between the door and the front picture window. The sheers were closed, but there was enough light to see through into the living room. That meant, however, that anyone who may be inside could see out as well, so I stayed low and close to the edge of the window. Other than the open door, there was no evidence that anyone else was around. There were no cars parked on the street for several blocks, but I knew that meant nothing. Bad guys who are smart won't park directly in front of a house where they're going to do evil. They park around the corner and up a few blocks, though not too far away, in case the need arises for a quick escape.

Looking around as best I could through the sheer drapes, everything looked for all the world like the inside of a house where people lived. As if the occupants were simply at work or out shopping for a new refrigerator. The coffee table didn't appear to be covered in dust and what appeared to be opened mail sat on it, though that could have been there for months, I guess. There was no sign of foul play, like a giant blood stain on the couch or a rotting corpse on the credenza in the dining room—no obvious reason for the smell, but I could only see most of the living room and part of the dining room beyond and to the left. A doorway on the right, which I guessed would lead to the kitchen, was too far to the right to see anything more than few feet of bare beige wall.

I didn't see any movement, but decided that it would be wise not to just walk in the front door, as being greeted by a hail of bullets from someone lying in wait would make it more difficult to pick up Dee at the airport. So I quietly retraced my steps back out the walk, across the drive and around the right side of the house, which had no windows on the ground floor since that whole wall was on the outside of the garage. At the back corner there was a chain link fence gate that had a lock on it, though the lock was open. I peeked around the corner into the tiny back yard that ended abruptly at the sheer rise to the railroad tracks after about twenty feet. There was a concrete patio that took up what appeared to be about half of the back yard. Closest to me was the back door to the garage. Beyond that about 15 feet was a sliding glass door that, if I figured right, opened into the dining room. On the patio were an ancient gas grill with tattered cover and a white five-piece patio set that appeared to be a match for the little round table on the front porch. There was no umbrella sticking out, though there was a small planter on top of the hole for it. The plant (a pansy, I think) in the terra cotta pot was alive and well, a product of the work of the lawn service, I assumed.

Quietly lifting the gate latch, I pushed it gently away from me, making sure it didn't squeak, just far enough to slide through. I sidled up to the wall right beside the garage door and put my back flat against it. I'm a lefty, but I put the gun in my right to make it easier to quickly dart my head past the door long enough to see if anything was moving inside. There was a dismembered body inside, but it was of a '65 Mustang. The car itself took up the left side of the garage, while the parts that had been removed covered the floor on the right, closest to the door into the house. Like my Ellie, this beauty was green. Unlike my Ellie, this was a fastback. The restoration had just gotten to the point of disassembly, though, so it was mostly just a chassis up on concrete blocks. I tried the door, but it was locked. I didn't want to alert anyone inside or get the cops called on me, so I opted not to break the glass.

I stepped between the patio table and the house and slid up to the edge of the door, repeating the quick glance to make sure there was no one there. There wasn't. Crouching down, I looked around at all I could see through the back door, which, as I had guessed, opened into the dining room, but it also looked into the kitchen on the left. I could see the part of the dining room that wasn't visible through the front window, but it revealed nothing new. Neither did

the kitchen. Nothing out of place, nothing indicating a crime had

been committed, no bodies with knives sticking out of them or with

a candle stick or wrench or rope or even a revolver beside them.

Nothing to explain the stomach-turning odor wafting from the front

door. The closest thing to something unusual was that the

refrigerator door was slightly open. That would make sense, though,

if the Tuttles had left and had the electricity turned off. Don't leave

the fridge shut to mildew. Somewhat more unusually, all of the

shelving had been removed and was leaned against the cabinets

beside the refrigerator. But they could have taken them out to clean

and just never put them back.

There was one more window at the far end of the house, so I

tried it. It was the master suite. The bed was made with a maroon

and green comforter and lots of pillows, the kind that took up half

the bed and I never understood why women wanted. To me a pillow

is something to put your head on so you can rest comfortably, not a

decoration. But I was lucky in that Dee never wanted lots of pillows

on our bed. Beside the bed on both sides were identical stands

holding identical lamps—brass with tiffany style shades. The only difference between the two tables was that the one on the left had an

electric clock radio. It showed no time, which meant there may not

be electricity in the house. On the wall opposite the bed was a

dresser with nothing on it save a flat screen television and its remote.

To the left of the dresser was a door that probably opened into a

walk-in closet. I studied the bedroom and bathroom, or what little I

could see of it, carefully, looking for anything that might be a clue.

Nothing.

Finishing the circle, I jumped the gate on the far side of the

house and walked around to the front again. There didn't appear to

be any movement anywhere. It didn't feel like there was anyone

there. After you've been doing this long enough, you become aware,

on an almost subconscious level, of the sound of a house that is

unoccupied. No odd creaks caused by someone walking upstairs. No

unexplained thumps from doors opening and closing. Just the sounds

of the house, if there are any. In this case there weren't even any of

those. Despite the fact that it was a sweltering day, the air

conditioning had never kicked on. Another indication that there may

be no electricity to the house.

I finally decided I had no choice but to go in through the front door. Gun in my left hand held up at eye level, I gently pushed on the door, an inch first, then a few more. The smell was nearly enough to make me vomit, but I had smelled worse and knew I probably would again, so I just ignored it and move on. It was clearly the smell of rotting flesh, but I had no reason to believe it was human flesh. At least not until I stepped around the corner into the kitchen and saw the dead body in the fridge. It had been dead for quite a while by the looks of it. I knew that the face was unrecognizable after a day or so, but this guy (and I only say guy based on the suit and tie) was well beyond that. He was bloated and covered with big blisters, which meant he'd been there dead for at least three or four days. He had probably been shoved in there and the door closed, but the swelling and expelled gases caused the door to pop open. I was careful not to touch anything after I saw the body. I didn't think it was Johnny, but it could have been practically anyone and I wouldn't have been able to tell. Whoever this was had on a black suit with a pink or peach pinstripe. It was hard to tell without opening the door further and risk having him pour out onto the floor. I could see his left hand and it had no wedding ring, though

I knew Johnny didn't wear his after he'd lost a large amount of weight. He always said he would get it re-sized someday, but that day never came, or at least it hadn't the last time I saw him. The hair was dark brown and looked to be a rug, but I didn't know if maybe that was an effect of the decomposition. Does your scalp slough off when you die?

After looking at the body as long as I could stand it, I looked around the rest of the house to see if there were any other bloaters inside of anything. The one in the fridge appeared to be the only surprise, but then again, one surprise like that in a day is quite enough.

Holstering my gun and using my elbow to nudge the door open further, I stepped out the front door to call the cops. But I didn't need to because there were already several there and they didn't seem happy. They were all pointing guns at me and they were shouting at me to drop to my knees and get my hands behind my head. I had been through this before, so I knew better than to try to explain who I was. I just put my hands behind my head and got on my knees, just like they said. When six cops are pointing guns at you, explaining won't help. Just let them make sure you aren't going to try to shoot them and then hope they let you explain after.

They did—after they patted me down. I had already told them about my gun and also about my PI credentials. They took the gun and ID, finished patting me down and asked me what I was doing there. I told them the short version and gave them the name and number of my friend, Sergeant Otis Campbell and said that he could vouch for me. Then a chunky officer with S. Crockett on his name badge put me in the back of a squad car, which smelled only a little bit better than the house. Someone had clearly relieved him or herself in the back of that car. Actually, I didn't want to know how many someones, probably, along with expelling who knows what other bodily secretions. I tried not to think about it too much as I watched the cops work their way into and back out of the house. They found the body just where I told them it would be. I could see one young looking guy retching a little as he staggered out the door. His first ripe corpse, I guessed.

Chapter 14

I told my story to the usual procession of cops, ending with a sergeant named Steve Dallas. He had called Otis and found that, and I quote, "'aside from being an occasional pain in the ass and not being nearly as funny as he thinks he is, he is okay.'" Dallas was tall and slim with jet black hair parted on the right. His nose was surprisingly long and slender, almost like Bob Hope's, though with no ski slope effect. It was uniformly straight, quite like a cartoon character nose. He wore dark reflective wrap-around sunglasses that sat funnily on his face because of the rod-like shape of his proboscis. I wondered as I looked at it if it grew when he told a lie.

The sergeant had not been involved in any of the work that Otis had requested, but he knew about it, so he was not surprised by the fact that I was there. As we finished, a member of the crime scene unit, a short, powerfully built young man whose dirty blonde hair was prematurely receding, came out the front door and walked directly to Dallas.

"We managed to get some prints off the stiff, though he wasn't really all that stiff. I guess he's more of a bloater, but nobody calls dead bodies bloaters, do they?"

I do, I thought.

"Anyway, Binkley," said Dallas, who had probably heard this guy ramble before.

"Yes, umm, anyway...his name is Milo Bloom. Or was. I guess his name still is that, though that's not really him anymore. If he is anymore. But that's not what we're talking about, is it?" Binkley took his silver-rimmed square glasses off and cleaned them with a cloth he had fished out of a pocket in his city-issued jumpsuit.

"Bloom is in the system, so he has a record, I assume," said Dallas.

"Just a bit." Binkley looked at his smart phone as he summed up Bloom's history. "Started his life of crime rather young. First arrest for shoplifting and possession at age 13. Graduated to car theft, then B and E, before his arrests started being associated with a mob enforcer named Rutger Stultz."

"Dingdingding—we have a winner!" I said, not realizing it had been out loud.

"A winner?" asked Dallas.

"That's the guy who tried to zip me. He's probably still trying to get the bees out of his head. My neighbor clocked him with the barrel of a 12-gauge and he's been goofy ever since."

"Bit of a coincidence," said Dallas.

I pulled my phone from my pocket to check the time. Holy crap—I was late to meet Dee at the airport! Her plane was scheduled to land in only half an hour. I explained to Dallas and he said he would be in touch and let me go.

Chapter 15

The traffic was with me and I got a parking space not quite a full mile from where I needed to go. As I dashed into the terminal, I looked for the arrivals board and was relieved to see that Dee's flight was going to land forty minutes late. I had time to catch my breath and grab a snack before she got there. I found myself in front of the Billy Goat Tavern & Grill, which I knew from the old *Saturday Night Live* sketches, so I stepped in for chezborger and Coke. Actually, I had a double cheeseburger, hold the bun, and an unsweetened iced tea—no fries or cheeps. I finished just in time to get to Dee's gate baggage carousel, which was good because I was too full to rush anywhere. I stopped and got a bouquet of flowers for my love and parked myself just outside of security so I couldn't miss her.

I stood excited as passenger after passenger walked by me, wondering when she would turn the corner and I would get to see that dazzling smile I'd missed for so long. My anticipation turned to anxiety as the last few stragglers went past and turned to full-blown panic when, ten minutes after the last person went by, I saw a couple members of the flight crew coming toward me. Either Dee was not on the plane or she hadn't gotten off the plane. Since I hadn't heard from her, either one of those scenarios would indicate something was wrong. So I stopped one of the flight attendants, a shortish brunette woman with a handsome face and too much makeup on.

"Excuse me ma'am."

"Yes sir," she replied, turning on her flight attendant smile. She had perfectly straight white teeth, made even whiter by her sun-darkened skin. When she smiled her face went from handsome to just plain pretty.

"I'm sorry to bother you, but my wife was supposed to be on that flight and I haven't heard from her. Is there any way she is still on the plane or something?"

She scrunched up her eyebrows for a second and bit the left side of her lower lip, struggling with whether she should trust me. Was I a stalker or an abusive husband trying to catch up to a woman who was running away? I tried to look as harmless as possible, but with my face it's a bit of a stretch to get harmless. I tried to think of myself as ruggedly handsome, but some would argue that I had plenty of rugged but not much handsome. Dee liked to call me Aslan because she said that I, like C. S. Lewis' powerful lion, may not be safe, but I am good. The pretty attendant with straight white teeth studied me for a few seconds and must have decided that I wasn't evil.

"What is your wife's name, sweetie?" Ah, a southern belle.

"Dee Shalan?" I raised my inflection at the end like it was a question. "Deanna Shalan, actually, but everybody calls her Dee." Shut up Shalan.

"I believe that's the name." The eyebrow scrunch coming back. "She's the reason we were late taking off. Waited as long as we could. Even called her name in the terminal, but she never showed up. Oh, honey, I'm so sorry, I hope she's okay."

I'd been shot at I don't know how many times (even been shot a couple times); while I'd rather not die, the thought of it never frightened me. The idea of something bad happening to Dee, though, petrified me. Why would she have missed that flight? And why didn't she call or text me to let me know? She was a compulsive texter, letting me know every little thing that was going on in her day, but it occurred to me that I hadn't heard from her all morning. I checked my phone to make sure, but I already knew that it had full signal and I hadn't received any calls or texts. "What can I do? Is there someone I can see to find out if she got a later flight?"

"Come with me." I followed her to a desk where a young man with a prematurely salt-and-pepper bottle brush moustache in the middle of a round face and body to match stood clicking on a computer keyboard staring intently at the screen. Before she could say anything, he held up one finger of his right hand and held it there as he typed and clicked with his left. We both waited patiently (well, maybe not patiently) as he finished whatever life-and-death task he was doing. I remember thinking that in about ten seconds I was going to snap that skinny white finger off his skinny white hand and stick up his doughy white nose. Luckily for us both, he dropped the hand and raised his sleepy grey eyes.

"How may I assist you?" he asked in a deep British accent.

"Hi…Basil," she said, reading his name tag. "This gentleman is looking for his wife who was supposed to be on my plane but didn't make it for some reason. I wonder if you'll be a dear and check for us to see if a Deanna Shalan got on or is booked on any flight from Cleveland to Chicago."

"It's Deanna Shalan, D-E-A-N-N-A, S-H-A-L-A-N," I added. I've always thought Shalan was a pretty easy name to spell, but had learned never to underestimate the mind's ability to add y's and e's and silent q's.

"I'm terribly sorry sir, but I have no record of either of those things. No one by that name is scheduled to fly anywhere from anywhere." Normally, I would take great delight in the fact that he said sheduled instead of scheduled. But not at the moment.

I'm a pretty resourceful guy, but I was frozen. I had no idea what to do. I tried calling her cell again—straight to voicemail. Her melodic lilt came on, told me to leave a message and I did, asking her to please call me. My heart felt like someone was squeezing on it and my stomach ached down deep, as if I had swallowed wet cement; I was pretty sure that if I didn't concentrate, I would throw up.

"I'm sure there's just something wrong with her phone, hon. Maybe she got sick," said the pretty redheaded attendant. She put her hand on my shoulder and tried to smile, but the concern was clear on her face.

Think, Shalan, think! Eventually, my mind emerged from the fog. We have an app that lets us see the GPS location of each other's phone. I thanked Basil and the attendant and checked the app—no good. Her phone was off. So I switched gears, sending an email to her phone with a signal word to turn it on. Going back to the locator app, I could see that her phone was still in Cleveland, but not at the airport. It was moving on Euclid Avenue, just passing the main campus of the Cleveland Clinic. I called it again.

"Hello?" The voice was decidedly not Dee's. It was decidedly not even a woman. Or if it was a woman, it was not any woman I would want to meet.

"Who is this?"

"Hello, Harry, and how you are this fine day?" He had a slight accent. German? Oh, crap.

"Where is my wife?"

"Your lovely wife loaned me her phone. She wasn't using it anyway. I admit I was taken aback when it rang. I'm quite sure I turned it off when she, um, handed it to me."

"What did you do with Dee, you piece of crap?!"

"Here, here, Harry, that's no way to treat the man who holds your lovely wife's fate in his hands."

"What do you want?"

"It's quite simple. All I need is your word that you are finished searching for Johnny Tuttle."

"I wouldn't have been looking for Johnny, you Teutonic twit, if you hadn't sent a bumbling crew of morons to try to kill me."

"We underestimated you, but we have much more efficient people at our beck."

I wasn't sure if he meant beck as in beck and call or back, as in *Young Frankenstein*. "Put ze candle beck." I guess it really didn't matter.

"So I can at least count on the next guy who tries to ice me knowing how to walk and chew gum at the same time?"

"Walk and--? I don't know what that means. At any rate, we call off our assassins, you drop the matter, yes?"

"If you give my wife back and stop trying to kill me, fine. But please answer one question."

"Why?"

"Yes why."

"I'm afraid that is, as I've heard you Americans say, far above my pay grade. We have your word, yah?"

"I'll drop it, but if you've harmed Dee in any way, I swear I will make you want to die for a long, long time."

"Your lovely wife is quite unharmed. She may have a slight headache after the sedative wears off, but I hope you won't consider that doing her harm. After all, we are not savages, are we? We may try to kill one another if the need arises, but to harm an innocent woman is the depth of depravity."

A hired killer with a code. I couldn't help but be a bit impressed. "What's your name?"

"Bernhard Stultz. Oh, and by the way, my brother Rutger is feeling better, no thanks to your brute of a neighbor."

"In his defense, your brother was trying to ventilate me at the time."

"Yes, there is that, I suppose."

Bernhard agreed to get Dee on the next flight after she was awake enough to travel on her own, promising to let me know when that would be. I hung up, wondering if I was being a sucker to believe this guy. Something in my gut told me that he was a man who lived by a code similar to mine, though his code allowed for cold-blooded murder.

I looked up and realized for the first time that this entire conversation, or at least my half of it, had taken place in front of Basil and the redhead, whose name, I now noticed, was Cybil.

"Found her, thanks."

Chapter 16

I found a café called Berghoff's and went in to have a cup of coffee. Perfect, Harry, a little caffeine to settle the nerves. I settled for half caf since it was getting late. A half hour and three cups later, my phone rang. It was Dee's number, but Bernhard was on the other end.

"Your lovely wife is awake now, and somewhat less than happy. I wonder if you'll speak with her and explain the situation?"

"I'll try."

I could hear a short exchange in which he told her it was me and she shouted my name several times. Her voice sounded a little bit ragged, as if the tranquilizer hadn't fully worn off.

"Harry? Harry, is that you?"

"Yes, babydoll, it's me. Are you okay? Did they hurt you?"

"Where am I who are these awful men where are you what's going on why are they doing this where are you come get me."

"Whoa honey, slow down, breathe. Now listen to me. Are you listening?"

There was a slight pause followed by simply, "Yes."

"Okay, these men are holding you because they want me to stop looking for Johnny Tuttle. I agreed to quit and they are going to let you get on a plane and come to Chicago to me. Is that okay or do you want me to come get you?"

"Come kill them! Come get me!"

"Sweetie, I'm not going to kill them, but I'll be glad to come get you, but you'll have to wait there for me. If you let them put you on a plane, you'll be away from them more quickly."

"But what if they kill me?"

"Bernhard promises you won't be harmed and I believe him. Now promise not to give them a hard time and not to run or call the police, and they'll put you on the next flight to Chicago, where I'll be waiting for you. Can you do that for me, Dee?"

There was another pause while she tried to process what I just told her.

"You promise let me go and not hurt me if I promise not to try to turn you in?" I heard her ask Bernhard.

"Yes, dear lady, we promise you'll be safe."

"Okay, I'll cooperate, but you are bad men! Very bad men!"

I chuckled to myself. These guys were in for some lecture.

Chapter 17

We said our goodbyes and she gave the phone back to Bernhard, who gave me his word that she would be safe and that he would return her phone to her before they left her at the airport, which he did, as witnessed by the text I received an hour later.

--They let me go. Waiting for my flight. Head pounding. Love you.

--Love you too. Sorry.

--Not your fault. I'm ok.

--You're amazing.

--I know. :-) Why did he believe we wouldn't tell?

-- Gave my word.

--He believed you?

--Mhm.

--And you believed he wouldn't hurt me because he said he wouldn't?

--Mhm.

--How did you both know?

--Hadn't hurt you yet. Could've killed you anytime. But he has a code.

--Like yours?

--Not exactly, but yes. Does what he says he will.

--He's a killer.

--Still has rules. His rules, but he won't break them. He's not good but you can trust his word.

--And you know this?

--Mhm.

--How?

--Spidey sense. :-)

--Seriously.

-- Just know. Read people. Part of why I'm good at this.

--Humble too. ;-)

--Is what it is. Everybody's good at something.

--Most people aren't as good at anything as you are at this.

--Blush.

--Is what it is.

--When is your flight?

--45 min. Boarding soon. There in about 90.

--Impatient.

--Not letting you out of my sight anymore. Get used to having a partner.

--Fine by me. Gun?

--Maybe. Let me think about it.

This was a major breakthrough. She didn't mind that I had to carry a gun in my job, and she was a surprisingly accurate shot at the range, but she refused to carry a gun, despite having a concealed carry permit. I bought her a Walther PPK for Christmas one year and she had become quite proficient with it. A better shot than I, to be honest, though that was against paper targets. Shooting at someone who is shooting at you is a slightly different situation. But, despite knowing that she was married to someone who occasionally had to make scary people mad enough to make attempts on my life, possibly in her presence, she never carried it. Aside from when she occasionally went to practice with me, it stayed in her night stand. I think it had more to do with her complete trust that I would be able to take care of her than with an aversion to the gun. I think she felt like it was my job to shoot the bad guys. I felt that too, but it's not

always that simple. There are many times when, even if you're
nearly superhuman, it's better to have two guns on your side.

We continued to chit chat, with the messages becoming more
and more lewd in nature, mostly consisting of what we intended to
do to and with each other when we got together in the hotel, but we
fell short of full-blown sexting, partly because we were both in
public and partly because her flight was called, so I was left to finish
in my mind, which I did. Knowing that I would need my strength, I
went back to the Billy Goat and ordered another chezborger.

I finished my snack and went to the men's room to splash
some water on my face. I would have loved to have a toothbrush, but
a stick of gum would have to do. I was excited to find Teaberry Gum
at a kiosk near her gate and bought some. Gum from one's childhood
tastes best. It's a rule.

Her flight arrived on time. I resisted the urge to run out,
climb up, and rip the door off the plane, but just barely. After
approximately a month, I could see the first person coming up the
jetway. I quickly unwrapped another piece of Teaberry and popped it
in my mouth. I was almost as nervous as on our honeymoon, nearly
strangling the life out of the bouquet I'd bought. After the first

person, a tall, thin, balding man who looked relieved to be off the plane, appeared, came a cute teenage girl with her long, straight, dirty blonde hair pulled back in a tight ponytail. She looked like an athlete, possibly a volleyball player based on her height. I always assume volleyball because it's my favorite sport to watch. As she ambled up the jetway, she accidentally ran the wheels of her carry-on up her heal and stumbled a little and as she veered to the left, the most startlingly beautiful face I had ever seen appeared. All other movement ceased. The cacophonous noises of the airport faded to a low mumble, drowned out by the thunder of my heartbeat. I experienced, as I have every time I've come into her presence, the familiar feeling of something falling into place in my soul, making it whole again.

Waiting for her to get to me, I became aware of the fact that I was bouncing on my toes. She didn't see me at first, but when she did, the smile exploded onto her face. Not a smile. The smile. The smile that made me ache in the back of my throat and nearly made me giddy.

I always thought it was completely cliché to say, but we melted into each other. When we hugged, it was like we became two parts of one whole. Finally surfacing, I became peripherally aware of movement around us, but that awareness was overwhelmed by the perfect texture of her hair and the ever-astonishingly sexual aroma of her perfume mixed with her natural scent. After hugging forever, we parted enough to look into each other's eyes and kissed lightly.

Without my becoming conscious of it, we began to walk (or, more accurately, glide) arm-in-arm to baggage pick-up. As we waited for the carousel to deliver her suitcase, we just stared at each other and smiled like idiots. Well, I smiled like an idiot—she smiled like the angel she is. We waited and waited, but eventually the carousel was empty. It finally dawned on us that her luggage had probably arrived on the original flight. After a short search, we found the unclaimed baggage office and claimed her luggage.

I kept waiting for her to get mad, but it never happened. Finally, when we were in the car and out of airport traffic, I asked.

"Well?" Ever eloquent.

"Well what, sweetie?"

"Are you okay?"

She thought that over a few seconds. "Okay doesn't quite cover it."

"Better than okay, or it's more complicated?"

"We've talked of what you do. I thought I understood it, what made you need to do it, to be who you are. But while this event scared me so completely that I thought I may literally wet my pants, it was also exhilarating in a way I've never known, like whitewater rafting combined with the fastest roller coaster ever plus a little of the day you proposed. And I understood that man. He was an awful, violent man, but I could see that there is something about him that makes him, on some level, like you. And being around him made me understand you more, respect you even more."

There are almost no people in the world whose opinion means much to me. My parents, of course, and siblings. Bull, and a few cop friends too. But no belief about me is more vital to my well-being than Dee's. To know that she saw me as worthy of such respect made me nearly float out of my seat. No words were sufficient, so I simply brought her hand, already clasped in mine, to my lips and kissed it gently several times, allowing myself to become intoxicated by the fragrance of her mixed with the joy of our reunion.

Chapter 18

We slept late the next morning despite getting back to the room early. It had been, shall we say, a pleasantly strenuous night that ended rather late with both of us sated sexually but famished, necessitating a rather expensive call for room service. Despite the sheer volume of food we both ate, neither of us had any trouble falling into a blissful slumber. In the morning, we spooned contentedly until we had to hurry to beat checkout time.

There was no rush to get home, so we stopped at our favorite Chicago eatery, Giordano's on East Lake Drive. We ordered our usual, a small stuffed shrimp pizza. Well, to call it our usual was probably a stretch. We'd gotten it once before and loved it so much that we agreed to get it again if we ever got back to the Windy City. Contrary to custom, we ordered coffee--black for me, half and half for her. And I don't mean half and half the coffee additive, but half cream and half coffee, plus sugar. Dee drank café lattes before they were cool. I, on the other hand, like my coffee like I like my women—full-bodied and strong. Normally, I think it the highest sacrilege to drink anything but beer, specifically Sam Adams, with pizza, or practically any meal after breakfast for that matter, but we were so late getting out of the room that neither of us had had any coffee.

For quite some time as we waited for our pizza, we sat in comfortable silence, holding hands and sipping our coffee. After a bit, though, her face became serious. I knew what she was going to ask.

"So is this over?"

"Looking for Johnny Tuttle?"

"Yes."

"I gave my word, so I have to stop actively searching for him. But he is my friend. I'll discreetly try to make contact. Anything more and we face the wrath of the Stultz brothers."

"You aren't afraid of them, are you?"

"For myself, no." I played with her wedding band and engagement ring with my thumb.

She smiled and the angels sang. "For me?"

"For them if they ever try to take you again."

The pizza came and all discussion ceased. Anyone who has eaten at Giordano's will understand.

Chapter 19

The day dawned brilliantly, though with a dark red timbre along the tops of the hills to the east. "Red in the morning, sailors take warning," I said to Dee as we walked from our house to City Park.

"Mhm," she said with a smile. This, I had learned over the years, was her way of saying she'd heard whatever I'd said a thousand times and was just humoring me with a response. I didn't mind. I had said that to her a thousand times. Probably every time I'd seen a red morning. I'd probably heard it twice that many times from my parents growing up, so it was baked right into me. Mostly it didn't bother me, though, because it was unseasonably warm, allowing Dee to break out her short running shorts. She could tell me where to stick my red morning and I wouldn't care as long as she was wearing short shorts.

It was a couple hours early, but we had a lot of eating to do that day, so we decided to go early and get in three easy miles before the Turkey Trot. Even at 7:00am, parking spots, especially near the pavilion where registration was taking place, were becoming hard to come by.

"Glad we walked," said Dee, dodging a black SUV going the wrong way. We stretched a little beside the gazebo near the park entrance, got a quick drink, and then began a slow jog around the park in silence. At our fastest pace, I'm a little faster than she is, but she has more stamina and can finish stronger in long races. We were both taking it easy on this day, though.

"Hold up," I said when I saw a bench coming up. My shoes felt uncomfortably tight, so I stopped to retie them. Dee bumped into me as I was tying the second. I thought she was being playful, but I saw she had jumped out of the way to avoid being clipped by the SUV again.

"Stupid SUV. You're going the wrong way!" They were long gone, though, and couldn't have heard her.

About halfway around the park, we were jogging past the left field fence of the baseball field. I could see the SUV we'd been dancing with parked in the tennis court lot about a hundred feet ahead on the right. I decided to give the driver, who was clearly not dressed for a run, a dirty look to let him know it wasn't okay that he nearly hit Dee. The longer I stared at him, though, the more I thought he looked familiar. Not like somebody I knew, but like somebody related to somebody I knew. But I couldn't place who. I guess my look worked, though, because the next time we came around, they were gone and we never saw them again. We finished one more lap, and then headed to the pavilion to register.

The saying proved to be true this time, as the temperature had dropped steadily until Dee regretted wearing such skimpy clothes. In the time it took to run the race, wait to hear we hadn't won a turkey for the eleventh consecutive year, and hustle back home, the sky had begun to darken, the wind had picked up, and the temperature had dropped at least ten degrees. By the time we'd showered and were headed to my parents' house, it had dropped another five and continued to plunge throughout the day in inverse proportion to the steadiness and velocity of wind. By the end of the Lions game, the bright blue sky of the morning had been replaced by threatening clouds and the relatively balmy temperatures at dawn had plummeted so that whatever fell from those clouds promised to be frozen. As the Cowboys and Dolphins kicked off, cold rain turned quickly to sleet. At halftime, which, by design, roughly coincided with dinner, the sleet had given way to hard ice pellets.

Mom announced that all was ready, so the family gathered upstairs to say grace and fill plates. With children, spouses, grandchildren with spouses or significant others, great-grandchildren, and our usual allotment of boyfriends, girlfriends, best friends, and various assorted folk who simply had nowhere else to be on Thanksgiving, there was no way we could even approach seating everyone around the table, even with all the leaves added and every seat that could be scrounged from other rooms wedged in. A card table in the living room and TV trays downstairs gave everyone a place to put their plates and drinks, but not in the same room or even on the same floor. The younger folks mostly went downstairs while the grown-ups gathered upstairs where we could talk.

Everything was set up, as it always had been, buffet style in the kitchen. A huge pot of green beans, home-grown in Dad's garden and home-canned by Mom, was on the stove, along with another pot, even bigger, full of Mom's famous homemade noodles. No diet could withstand the intoxicating allure of those glorious, starch-laden beauties. Moving to the right the counter was covered with turkey, already carved by my brother the butcher. Beside the turkey were baked ham, garlic-cream cheese smashed potatoes, homemade dressing, jugs of tea, two-liters of pop, a large bowl of ice, and a green salad with various dressings. On the kitchen table were homemade rolls and squaw bread, butter, home canned jam and apple butter, a tray of pickles and olives (including home canned bread-and-butter pickles made from cucumbers grown in Dad's garden), a vegetable tray, and a fruit tray. The counter on the other side of the room was home to the desserts, all, again, made from scratch: two pumpkin pies, pecan pie, cherry pie, fruit cake, cheesecake, and about seven different kinds of cookies. Even considering the mass of humanity that pushed my folks' comfortably large home to capacity, it was a decadent amount of food.

Mom found me in the throng, slipped her arm around my waist and said it was time for grace. As it is my brother's job to carve the roast beasts, it is my appointed position to pray at all family gatherings.

"Let's pray everybody." Dee had stolen up beside me without my noticing and took the hand that wasn't over Mom's shoulder. All was right with the world. Until my phone rang.

"Sorry!" I silenced my phone and started the prayer. "Dear God, we humbly thank you for this holiday and its reminder just how much we have been blessed. Thank you for this food and for the loving hands that prepared it. In Jesus' name, amen."

I squeezed the two women I love most in the world and let Mom go back to her accustomed job of overseeing the progression of the feast. She was the last to eat, no matter how we all protested that her work was finished and she should be the first in line. She, being Mom or Nana to everyone, had to make sure all was well and all were fully fed before she could sit down for the first time since before dawn.

Dee and I wandered from the living room toward the kitchen for the first plate load. Well, to be fair, it was Dee's first and last, unless you count dessert. It was my first, but definitely not my last. They don't make a plate large enough to get an adequate helping of all the foods I have to eat in order for it to count as a successful Thanksgiving dinner. I have considered using a garbage can lid as a plate, but I don't want to be seen as a pig. I apparently don't mind being a pig, but being seen as one is problematic. I tell myself a six-mile jog will negate the thousands of calories I eat that day, but deep down I know I'm lying to myself. And I'm okay with that.

Two plates of dinner plus slivers of pumpkin pie, pecan pie and cherry cheesecake later, I felt roughly the shape of Violet from *Charlie and the Chocolate Factory* after she chewed the gum. Dee was still working on her only plate of dinner. I could roast and eat most of an entire turkey in the time it took her to eat a small plate of food. It's partly that I'm a fast eater, due in part to my time as a teacher, but the reality is that she almost certainly was the slowest eater in the history of the world. She took a bite, put down her utensil, chewed for what seemed like a minute or two, swallowed, talked with the people around her, and took a couple sips of her iced tea before picking up her fork again. All this while I'm polishing off two plates, three hot rolls, and dessert. People watch her carefully just to make sure she's still moving. They watch me while I eat to guard against accidentally getting swept up in the maelstrom.

I left Dee at the table to refill my iced tea and step outside to cool off. The furnace wasn't running, but the house was filled to the top with people, each adding body heat. As I opened the front door, I was blasted in the face with an icy gale and noticed for the first time that the ice pellets from before dinner had given way not just to snow but to blizzard conditions. Snowflakes, many as large as tennis balls, were hammering down at such a rate that the cars parked in the street, a mere twenty feet away, were nearly invisible. The ground was already completely covered over and I knew that the ice that had fallen earlier would make walking or driving highly treacherous. Luckily, we had brought Eddie, who was busy moving from person to person begging turkey and ham, with us, so we would probably crash here for the night. We had driven Dee's Escape, but it didn't look worth risking it. I sat on the porch swing for a few minutes watching the snowstorm, surprised to find that it was actually gaining in intensity; as I rose to go back in, I was startled by a clap of thunder in the distance.

"It's a whiteout folks!" I pushed the front door closed. "Just heard thunder. Hope nobody needs to be anywhere tonight."

"Hope we don't run out of food," said my sister Penny with a smile.

"I think we'll be safe, at least until morning," said Will, my brother. "It seems like the turkey and ham I carved were about 25 pounds apiece."

Flopping on the couch beside Penny, I rubbed my distended belly. There were no seats left, so Dee, who had skipped dessert for the time being, came and curled up on my lap, putting her head on my shoulder. It hurt my stomach, but it was worth it. I wrapped my arms around her slender shoulders and kissed her forehead a few times. She responded with a contented sigh.

The conversation lulled as everyone struggled to stay awake. Half asleep, I started as my phone vibrated in my pocket. The screen informed me that I had seven missed calls. I guess it took Dee sitting on my lap for me to notice the vibration. Who would have called me seven times in such a brief span, though? I didn't recognize the number, but could see it was a Chicago area code. My heart fluttered a little. I didn't notice at first, but whoever had called had also left three voicemails.

"What's wrong?" Dee could see the concern on my face. I showed her the phone. It took a few seconds, but the area code registered and her eyes widened.

"Is it--?"

"I don't know."

I pulled up the first voicemail.

"Harry? Harry, this is John Tuttle!" The voice was unmistakably Johnny's, though he was obviously whispering and on the edge of panic. "I need your help. Please call me as soon as you can. PLEASE!"

I hit play again and put it up to Dee's ear. As she listened, her mouth formed an O and she stared at me in horror.

"Oh, Harry…"

"I know."

The second message was a repeat of the first with just a bit more panic. The third was chilling.

"HARRY, WHERE ARE YOU?! Oh, God, please help—no, get away from me!"

There were sounds of a struggle and a muffled thud that I presumed was the phone hitting the floor or ground. Then nothing. We had listened together with our heads touching. I could feel Dee quivering. Johnny was in bad trouble at best. I didn't want to think it, but it could already be too late. I called the number back, but it went straight to voicemail. Probably off.

I called Otis Campbell's cell number. It rang five times before going to voicemail. I hung up and dialed again. This time it went to voicemail after the second ring. The schmuck rejected the call! He had to know better. I called again. Finally realizing the hopelessness of his situation, he answered.

"It's Thanksgiving, leave me alone!"

"I'm sorry, but it's an emergency. Johnny Tuttle called me."

It took a few seconds. It had been five months since we got back from Chicago and four months since we'd both given up on contacting him.

"Tuttle! You sure it was him?"

"No question and he was in a panic."

"Where is he?"

"No idea. He left voicemails."

"Call him back?"

"Gee, wish I'd thought of that. It's off. Can you trace the cell from which the call came?"

"From which the call came? I always feel like such a moron when I talk to you."

"Go with that feeling. Can you?"

"Yeah. Number?"

I gave him the number, which he repeated back to me after a brief pause and said he'd call back.

Thanks. Happy Thanksgiving."

"Bite me."

Chapter 20

While we waited for Otis to call, Dee and I, both needing something to occupy ourselves, helped Mom clear the dishes from all over the house and put away leftovers. It felt like an hour, but in reality it was only about fifteen minutes before my phone rang.

"You won't believe it," said Otis.

"Who is this?"

"Shut up. Call routed through a cell tower less than half a mile from your address. He could've been in front of your house."

"He's here in town?"

"The call definitely originated from here."

"Thanks, Otis. Owe you one."

"I'll add it to your account."

We hung up as I headed to the coat closet in the hallway. Dee followed me.

"Johnny's here?"

"The call likely originated within sight of our house. I have to go home and see if he's there."

"But the roads!"

"I'll be careful. If it's too slick I'll hoof it. It's just over a mile."

"I'm going."

"You aren't dressed for the hike if I do get stuck."

"I can loan her some warmer clothes and boots," said my mom. I hadn't realized she was standing there.

"You and I are partners, remember? I need to do this."

She had helped with cases for the last few months, but nothing approaching dangerous. Surveillance, phone calls, research, knocking on doors; the boring, safe stuff. Nothing where gunplay was likely. But we had agreed.

"Okay. Did you bring your Walther?" I asked Dee, who was already in my parents' room changing clothes.

"It's in the console of the Escape, right beside your gun!" There was excitement in her voice, but my stomach was filling with magma. There was every chance of danger, something I walk into regularly without thinking much about it. Sure, I'd rather not die, but in my line of work, you learn to put fear in a box and set it aside; I wasn't sure I could box up the fear I was feeling at this moment. It was rising up my spine and threatening to shut off my brain. I tried to calm myself, first by going out and starting and digging out the Escape and second by reminding myself that she was at least as good a shot as I was and that she was a brown belt in Tae Kwon Do. She was also, unlike me, willing to admit when she was in over her head and either get help or run. She was probably better equipped for this job than I was.

She being sufficiently dressed and I being sufficiently soothed, we set off. The vehicle hadn't warmed up enough to make a difference in the internal temperature, so our breath came out in clouds, which helped me see that she was breathing pretty heavily.

"Deep breaths, in through the nose, out through the mouth. You're ready for this."

"I know I'm ready! I'm just excited—this is the first time you've let me off the leash!"

"I wouldn't necessarily say off the leash. Maybe a longer leash."

"Potato, potahto. I finally get to really be your partner."

Our conversation was cut short as we hit the bottom of the long, winding hill that led out of my parents' neighborhood. I got no more than about twenty yards up it before completely losing traction.

We stopped moving and then slowly slid back to the bottom of the hill, coming to rest against the curb in front of Mrs. Addams' house. I wasn't surprised, but had hoped we would luck out.

"Looks like we're hiking," said Dee, reaching into the console to retrieve her weapon. I got mine and dropped it in my coat pocket.

"We might be better off," I said, "going overland instead of following the roads. It's a direct shot through neighborhoods to our house. I imagine it'll be easier to walk through people's yards than on the streets anyway."

So off we went, first through Mrs. Addams' yard, then along the edge of the woods behind an apartment complex, eventually going along what is usually a path in the woods, though, aside from the fact that there was a slight gap in the trees, there was no path evident. The snow, still falling heavily, occasionally picked up pace and, when an especially strong wind gust hit, flew horizontally, blinding me temporarily. The temperature had continued to drop, but we didn't take long to warm up and start loosening layers. The snow was nearly a foot deep and quite dense due to the water content, making the walking laborious. I did most of the heavy lifting by breaking a trail, allowing Dee to stay in my tracks.

After about twenty minutes, we broke out of the woods at Cashman Street at the top of a small hill. Dropping down the hill along the street for a couple blocks, we then cut up a sidewalk that was put through the middle of the neighborhood so students would have a shortcut walking to school. The sidewalk was a slight uphill grade, which would not be a problem in decent weather, but the thickness of the snow combined with the whipping snow and wind made for slow, laborious progress. I stole occasional glances back at Dee. Her breath came out in large plumes of vapor, but it was not heavier than it should have been and her face was stony and resolute. I saw no hint of fear. That made one of us.

The sidewalk finally ended at the street that meandered down into our neighborhood. If the weather weren't so foul, I could have seen the soft white Christmas lights in the shrubbery at the front of our house. I paused there, partly to let Dee catch up, but also to catch my breath and think about how to proceed. We could march down there in the middle of the street since there was literally no traffic, but I had to account for the possibility that whoever had done whatever they did to Tuttle might still be around. In a few seconds, Dee was standing beside me wiping the snow that had accumulated off her torso and arms.

"So what's the plan?" she asked.

"I hadn't really come up with one yet, though I thought it might be best not to just walk down the middle of the street."

"Yeah, somebody might be waiting for us. Or maybe they're stuck in the snow, but either way, we don't want to be sitting ducks."

"That's impressive."

"Well, thank you!" She smiled broadly. "You may not believe it, but I do listen to what you say when you talk to me about your work."

"Okay, then, what do you propose?"

"Well, how about we cut through back yards until we get to the end of the alley that leads to the back of our place. The fencing and trees should shelter us until we get nearly to our house. At least close enough to get a look around. The snow will help hide us a little, at least."

"Sounds like a plan."

So that's what we did. After about twenty minutes, we were crouched at the edge of the fence that ran between our house and the one next door. Although there was a small gap between the fence and our hedge, in order to keep from exposing ourselves too much, we had to stop in a place where our view was partly obstructed, but it was clear that something had happened back there. A large portion of the hedge on the far end of the yard had been driven through by a Humvee or something of a similar size, the porch railing outside our back door was broken again, and tire tracks all the way up to the back of the house were still evident, though the snow had made a good start on filling them back in.

Dee shook her head after taking in the scene. "Man, Mr. Williams is going to kick us out for sure this time."

"How do we know this even has anything to do with us? It could be a coincidence,"

"You know what Gibbs says about coincidences."

"This isn't *NCIS*."

"Do you think this is one?"

"Nope. These guys came after Tuttle."

We watched for evidence that anyone was lying in wait. After a minute or two, I reached down, scooped up a chunk of snow, and rolled it into a grapefruit-sized snowball. Stepping through the hedge, I fired the snowball toward the house and stepped back. The snow was wet and heavy enough that it made quite a loud splat as it exploded against the back of the building just beneath Mr. Williams' back window. No one moved. We couldn't wait there much longer unless we were willing to build an igloo for warmth, so I stepped through the gap between the fence and hedge followed by Dee. Staying low, we hurried along the fence, then split up and circled the house. Meeting at the front porch, we found the yard and the street beyond to be peaceful and pristine. Under other circumstances I would have found the scene blissful, but at the moment I was concentrating on more pressing matters. We headed back and followed what was left of the tire tracks down the alley opposite of the way we came in. After two blocks, the alley emptied out onto Matheny Drive. Turning right on Matheny, which is what the people who mowed down our hedge appeared to have done, would lead to City Park, and then almost anywhere.

Having no effective way to follow or know where they went even if we could, we decided there was nothing else to do but go inside and get warm. The back stairs looked like a giant snowdrift, so we went around to the side door leading to a narrow interior staircase. Shedding our snowy outside clothes and leaving them at the bottom landing, we headed up the steps. As I hit the bottom of the last flight, I froze. A shaft of light showed through a gap between our front door and the frame—the door was slightly ajar. Dee didn't notice I had stopped and ran into me, emitting a loud "OOF!" I pivoted quickly, raised my gun, and put my left hand over Dee's mouth to stop any further sound. At first, her eyes appeared puzzled, then angry, and then grew wide with understanding. I urged her back around the corner out of view of the door and put my mouth to her ear.

"Door is open. Wait here. Be ready."

She nodded gravely, though I could tell she was finally a little shaken. I kissed her cheek and headed down the steps. At the bottom landing sat a flat broom and a push broom. I opted for the flat broom. Broom in hand, I crept back up the stairs to where Dee waited. Seeing what I was carrying, she tilted her head quizzically.

Handing her the broom, I raised one finger to signal that she would understand in a second. I got down on my hands and knees and crawled around the corner to the bottom of the stairs. Reaching back around me, I held out my hand. Dee understood and handed me the broom, bristles first. Good girl. I snaked the broom up the steps, making sure to keep it just barely above the steps until the head was just at the door. Holding my breath, I fired the broom as hard as I could against the door, not worrying anymore about being quiet. The door swung open and rattled against the wall inside the apartment. It was at this point that things got a little wild.

A dark figure, silhouetted against the light from inside the apartment, came bellowing down the steps at me. I stood up against the wall to let him get past me and stuck my foot out to trip him. He careered past me and crashed on the landing below. Dee let out a scream and leapt onto his back. Not what I expected.

"Freeze, hairball!"

I actually snorted I laughed so hard.

"I don't think he's going anywhere, sweetie." I pulled her off the crumpled mass.

"Uhhhh…Dee," said the semi-conscious man with a moan.

"What the frack?" said Dee in surprise.

Knowing the voice, I rolled him over. It was swollen and marred by cuts, blood, and bruises, but there was no mistaking the face of Johnny Tuttle.

Chapter 21

Dee checked him over and declared him to be in no immediate danger, so we helped him upstairs and deposited him on the couch, where he fell dead asleep for almost four hours. Dee checked on him from time to time to make sure he was still breathing, but mostly left him alone. It was nearly midnight when he finally came around.

"Happy Thanksgiving," I said when he staggered into the kitchen and joined us at the bar.

"Dear me, it's Thanksgiving. I completely forgot. Well, that I have finally gotten to you is something to be thankful for."

"Question—why did you put a hit out on me?"

"Ah, yes, I forgot about that too. Sorry about that. Long story. If it's any compensation, I didn't really want to. I needed you to come and hopefully pull my fat from the fire, but I didn't know a way to get in touch without raising alarms with some rather bad people."

"Hiring someone to kill me is an odd way to get my help. I can't help you dead.

"Well, it was the best I could come up with under the circumstances. I knew you to be hard to kill and someone who would not likely gun me down or haul me in to the police without finding out why I, of all people, had put a hit on you. And, frankly, even if you wouldn't listen, at least turning me in would have gotten me away from those who controlled me. Besides, I asked specifically that they send Rutger Stultz and his band of misfits after you. He's not as bright as you might think, unlike his brother."

"Okay, wait," I said, "we seem to be approaching this thing from the wrong end. How about you start at the beginning?"

"As I said," he replied, "it's a long story and it's quite late, isn't it? What time is it, anyway?"

"It's a little past midnight," said Dee. "But we have nowhere to go. When was the last time you ate?"

"Hmm, I had a protein bar this morning sometime. Or maybe it was yesterday morning. What day is it? Ah, yes, Thursday—well, Friday now. But regardless, I now realize that I am famished."

"Well then," said Dee, "we'll fix something while you get cleaned up. You look like you could use a shower and some clean clothes.

"That sounds amazing," said Tuttle. "We've been on the run for so long that I don't remember the last time I ate an actual home-cooked meal."

After rummaging through my dresser drawers to find something that would not be too awfully large for Tuttle, Dee and I started working. I decided on some turkey hash using leftovers from dinner with Dee's family the day before and she on biscuits. Kneading the dough in a clear glass bowl, she blew a stray lock of auburn hair out of her chocolate eyes and looked up at me.

"What do you think?"

"I'm not sure what happened." I used my left index finger to wipe a spot of flour from her pixie nose and then gently kissed the very tip. "But I know he meant me no harm."

"You know him that well?"

"I know my gut that well."

"Your famous gut." She poked my belly and kissed me fast on the lips.

After that, we worked quietly on our midnight snack. In an impressive feat of timing, Tuttle appeared as the last item hit the table. He looked considerably happier than he had when we found him in a crumpled heap at the bottom of our staircase. Well, to be fair, we put him in the crumpled heap, but that was hardly our fault. He being a couple inches taller and about 40 pounds lighter than I, my sweat shirt was pretty baggy on him and the pants were a bit short. But he was clean and clearly hungry based on the almost fiendishly ravenous way in which he looked over the well-laden table. I almost expected him to rub his hands together and give out an evil cackle. But he controlled himself.

"Sorry I was so long. Bit stiff and sore. Hope you don't mind, but I used some Band-Aids and ointment out of your medicine cabinet. Oh, and I used your phone to call Lilith to let her know I'm alive."

"Where is Lilith anyway?" I asked.

"Close by, safe." It seemed a cryptic answer, but I let it pass.

"No worries," answered Dee. "We just got this on the table. Please—sit, eat."

No more invitation was needed. He lit into his plate with as much fervor as propriety would allow. Dee and I smiled at each other and ate. I wish I could say that I wasn't hungry after our huge Thanksgiving feast, but I don't like to lie. I was starving. Not the way Johnny was, though. I was pretty certain that, if we hadn't been there, he would have been using his bare hands to shovel the food in. After giving him a chance to catch up on his breathing and swallowing, I reminded him he owed us a story.

"Yes, well, where to begin?

Chapter 22

"It all began some five years ago," he said between bites. "Five years last September, in fact. I was teaching at Northwestern. In fact, that's where the problem started. Lilith and I were happy together; we both enjoyed Chicago. I loved my position and the prestige of teaching at an academic powerhouse like NU.

"But life for me had become somewhat like Hamlet's: weary, stale, flat, and unprofitable. I taught, I had office hours, I wrote a few mediocre books that nearly no one read, I went to school functions like a good professor should, often wishing I drank more; we talked often of traveling abroad between semesters, but she was busy starting up a business and volunteering with Habitat For Humanity, so we couldn't even do that very often. I suppose I lost my spark, my joie de vivre. I mean, when I grew bored before, I moved on and up. Find a better school, a better position. But what's better than Northwestern? I looked into Harvard and Stanford; Harvard wouldn't have me and I had no interest in moving to the left coast. So I was stuck, or at least I felt that way.

I was getting sleepy, so I cleared the table, put leftovers in the refrigerator, and scraped dishes before putting them into the dishwasher. Dee seemed absorbed in the story, but I was pretty sure she was just acting like that so she wouldn't have to help.

"Then one day, my neighbor asked me to get into a football pool. It was nothing—ten dollars. It was one of those where you have a number for each team and there was a payout at the end of each quarter and the end of the game. Bobby Harlow, my neighbor had invited me to join in nearly every week since we moved there, but I just never saw the use in frittering away even ten dollars on gambling. I would rather have put the money away for a rainy day. I guess the boredom had gotten to me, though, and I had just been thinking about the fact that we had enough to get us through several rainy days. So I got a wild hair and gave him the money.

"Did you win?" Maybe Dee really was absorbed in the story.

"Well, yes and no." He stared off into nothing for a few seconds before continuing. "I have never been a huge fan of football, college or otherwise, but even I knew when he gave me my numbers that I had experienced an instance of beginner's luck."

"Don't tell me," I said as I sat back at the table, "seven and three."

"Seven and three indeed. It was seven to three at the end of the first, second and third quarters, and then both teams went on a scoring binge in the fourth quarter, but the final score, insanely enough, was seventeen to thirteen. So I won the entire pot. One thousand dollars.

"A thousand dollars!" Dee shook her head. "How lucky!"

"I wager you'll think differently soon, pun intended." He downed the last of what had to be room temperature coffee. "It wasn't as if I needed it—as I mentioned, we've always been cautious with our money and I could have retired whenever I wanted, but, as I said, Lilith was busy and I don't enjoy writing enough to do it full-time. But when I won that pool, it was like a jolt of electricity went through me. It was like Christmas, New Year's, and my birthday all rolled into one. I felt adrenaline, I swear to God, like I hadn't felt since my first time with Lilith. And she was my first. My only. I mean, it was like I'd been walking around wearing glasses that made the whole world gray and suddenly I took them off to find that everything around me was in dazzling Technicolor.

"I'm not sure I've ever experienced that," said Dee.

"I have," I said with a wink as I squeezed her hand. She blushed and smiled shyly.

"I didn't know what to do with it." He was so caught up in telling his story that I wasn't sure he even heard us. "You know me—I have rules I live by. I am terminally responsible. But seriously, I felt like my heart had been asleep and was beating, really beating, for the first time in I don't know how long. I agonized over it for days, but I finally convinced myself this was found money, so it could hardly hurt anything if I bet it and lost. I would even pull out the original ten dollars so the worst that would happen would be that I would come out even. I should've known that it was wrong just by the fact that I couldn't bring myself to tell Lilith about it. I was excited beyond words, but a little ashamed too, and even a little scared by how out of control I felt. But excited won—I'm sad to say it won by several lengths."

"So you bet a horse race?"

"I take it that's a horse racing term?" asked Dee. I nodded, but he rolled on without hesitation, still nearly oblivious to our input.

"The next Saturday, Lilith was off doing something to do with Habitat, so I went to Arlington Park. As I said, I wasn't a huge fan of football, but at least I know the game. I do not exaggerate, however, when I say I knew nothing, and I mean nothing, about horse racing, much less about handicapping it. But I bet every penny. On one horse. I just looked at the lineup and found a horse with a name that jumped out at me. I still remember it. Spenser's Faerie Queene. Can you imagine that?"

"I don't get it." Dee looked from him to me and back.

"Sir Edmund Spenser wrote *The Faerie Queene*. I read it for his class my sophomore year. And he's the namesake of Robert B. Parker's detective, all of whose books we've both read at least twice."

"Me a literature professor and a Parker fan besides. How could I not? So I laid $990 on her to win. She was probably one race from the glue factory based on the odds—20:1. I half expected her not to have four legs, or to have been named after Queen Elizabeth because she'd ridden her once. But she looked like a horse. A regular horse, just like the rest. And it turns out this was her day, which meant it was mine as well. She hit the first turn in third place, but she worked her way out from the pack about halfway through the back stretch. Suddenly, it was like somebody had strapped an Atlas rocket to that horse, because she took off so fast it looked like the other horses had stopped in their tracks. She didn't just win—she won by almost fifteen lengths. She could have stopped and moon walked the last few lengths and still won."

"You bet almost a grand at twenty to one?" I struggled to do the math, but knew it was just shy of twenty thousand.

"Yes. I walked to the window in a daze. It didn't seem real. When I handed the young fellow my ticket, he looked at it, then at me, then at the ticket and back again. I could hardly blame him for being suspicious—a bet that size on a horse that should never have won. Betting on her to show would have been a fool's wager. But she won. I won. How could they not suspect the race was fixed? I could barely believe it myself and it was I who laid the bet. He said something to me, though I have no idea what. My ears, along with the rest of my faculties, seemed to be stunned into uselessness. With a thick tongue and benumbed mouth, I mumbled some nonsense about the horse's name and the fact that I was an English professor. I had no idea if that was even an appropriate response to whatever he said. He could have been asking me how I liked the weather. He squinted at me, shook his head a little, and stepped away from the window. It barely registered that he was gone before he came back. I assume in retrospect that he was checking with somebody with the authority to make such a payoff or some such. He quite likely lacked the requisite funds in his till to hand it over in one lump sum. It didn't even occur to me until afterward to worry that they wouldn't give it to me without questioning me to see if I had cheated somehow. I don't know how long he was gone, but he eventually showed up and gave me my money. One-hundred-and-ninety-eight $100 bills."

"That's almost twenty thousand dollars." Dee shook her head, her eyes wide.

"It's a miracle I wasn't robbed because I realized when I got to my car that I had carried the stack of bills in my hand the whole way and I'm sure I must have seemed tipsy or drug-addled.

"So I had placed two bets in just over a week and, literally through no fault of my own, turned ten dollars into almost twenty large. Twenty large. That's a term I'd never even heard before then.

It never sounded right coming from me. I mean, for the love of all that's good, I was just a mousy little college professor."

"I take it your subsequent bets didn't go quite so well." I stretched in my chair, trying to work out a kink in my low back.

"That could be the understatement of the century. It was like I had used up all my luck in one fell swoop. Well, two fell swoops, to be more precise. I wish my luck had ended after that first bet. Who knows—if I'd lost the bet on the horse, I may well not be in this mess. Sometimes it seems like God has a cruel sense of humor. But, I bet on anything and everything after that. As it happens, I really stink at gambling. Actually, stink doesn't do it justice. People who actually do stink at gambling would make fun of me. A new word would have to be invented to fully describe my inability to bet efficaciously. I'm not sure I won even one other wager from that day to this. The hell of it is, I would give my right arm to do it again, and I haven't placed a bet in years. This whole gambling jag lasted but a few months, though that was long enough to ruin my life."

Dee gently placed her left hand on his right shoulder and squeezed it lightly. He looked at her wistfully and patted her hand with his.

"It took me all of another week to burn through my initial winnings, playing horses, football pools—big ones—football games themselves—anything that I could persuade someone else to bet on. I even remember betting some random person my last thousand on a coin flip. A coin flip. I swear I could have supplied the coin, made it two-headed, and called it myself and the cursed thing would have come up tails."

"A thousand on a coin flip?" Even I was shocked.

"I tried to stop after that, but I just couldn't. In a few months, our savings was gone and I cashed in our money market accounts and both IRAs. When that money was gone, I took out a home equity loan, a second mortgage, and then borrowed everything I was allowed against my retirement. That was gone in less than another month. I had no money. I hocked anything I could sneak out of the house. But that ran out quickly as well, so I told Lilith I was going green and wanted to sell my car and take the bus to work. She thought that was odd, but she went along with it. I blew it all, plus another three thousand dollars that I didn't have, on a Bulls game. I told my bookmaker that I had a feeling about the game and wished that I could bet more; he was nice enough to extend me a loan. That was the first time I bet money I didn't have. I wasn't daft enough to think he was actually being nice or that I would have any way of paying back even the vig—another word I'm ashamed to have learned—let alone the loan itself. All I knew was that I had to win."

"Vig?" Dee looked at me.

"Vigorish. Interest. High interest."

"I watched the game in a bar in a part of town where I thought I wouldn't run into anyone I knew. It was, to put it politely, a dive, a place I would never have been caught dead in just a few months earlier. I got an odd look from the bartender when I ordered a glass of iced tea and nursed it, along with about a hundred bowls of bar mix, the whole game, but the horrible truth is that I lacked the funds for anything else. Thank God for free refills. The Bulls led comfortably the entire game. I remember the exhilaration of believing that this was the bet that was going to turn my luck around."

"You actually thought you could gamble your way out of the hole?" I asked incredulously.

"I've since found through Gamblers Anonymous that this is typical. I was completely convinced that my problem wasn't that I was addicted to gambling but that I'd just had a bad run of luck and all I needed was one break and things would go my way. I could replace all the money I'd wasted and Lilith would be none the wiser. She must have known something was amiss, but hadn't any idea how awry things had gone." He got up and began pacing, a tricky proposition in our rather undersized apartment. "At any rate, going into the fourth quarter, the Bulls were up by fifteen on the Lakers. I can see it in my mind just like I'm there again, watching on the TV in that seedy bar. I can even smell the cigarette smoke and stale beer in the air, along with the stench of my own desperation and depravity. Kobe Bryant had been off the whole game, but he seemed to come to life with the opening whistle of the final quarter. They just chipped away and chipped away. The Bulls didn't stop scoring, but Bryant just went insane. They tied the game with twenty seconds to go on one of the most beautiful alley oops I'd ever seen from Jordan Farmar to Kobe.

"Alley oop?" Dee looked at me, beginning to lose patience with terms she didn't know.

"Basketball term." She frowned, shrugged, and turned back to Tuttle.

"It just about crushed my soul, but by some miracle Ben Wallace got open underneath with nine seconds left. He slammed it home and got hacked. Odom fouled out. Wallace hit the foul shot and I was nine seconds from payday. The worst that could happen was overtime, but what were the odds in five seconds?"

"I think I actually remember that game," I said. "Ran on Sportscenter for weeks. Won some Espies. Kobe won the game with a four-point play, didn't he?" Tuttle looked like he'd just swallowed a bug. I really need to learn to shut up.

"I was up putting my coat on to head out and find my bookie when it happened. It's so real, still to this day in my mind, though it seemed like a horrible phantasm at the time. I assume the Bulls believed the game to be over as well, because Andrew Bynum caught the ball as it fell through after the foul shot, stepped out of bounds, and fired the ball to Kobe at quarter court. Kobe dribbled over half court and was at about thirty feet away along the sideline when he pulled up for a desperation three. Luol Deng rushed to get a hand in his face, but he tripped and rolled into Bryant as the shot left his hand. The referee blew the whistle for a foul and raised his hand to signal a three-point attempt just as the horn sounded and the ball caromed straight up from the front of the rim, came down on the back of the rim, bounced off the backboard and fell through for the tying points. My crushed soul, only just beginning to breathe again, was bathed in napalm and set ablaze. My only hope was for Kobe to miss the free throw and for the Bulls to somehow reverse the momentum in overtime, but the shot was one of those perfect swishes that barely even disturb the net. It was over. The game was over. My gambling career was over. The chances of my luck ever turning were over. Life as I knew it was over. Since I knew I had no chance of paying my debt, I had every reason to believe that my life was soon likely to be over."

He stopped pacing at the back door and stared silently for a minute out into the still driving snow. I pulled Dee up by the hand I had been holding and led her to the couch, where I sat and she laid down, her head on my lap. He continued without turning back to us.

"I just sat there staring at the screen. No idea how long I was in that catatonia. The thought that ran on a loop through my head was that I had nothing. I mean nothing. In actuality, I had less than nothing. I had sold or cashed in everything I could without coming clean to Lilith. And I'd lost it all. Every single penny. The one item of value that I still had left was our house, and we had two mortgages and an equity loan against it, so we were hopelessly upside down on it, not to mention the fact that I had no hope of even making the payments on it, which meant we would almost certainly be losing that to the bank in a few short months. If it weren't for having money left on my Chicago Card, I wouldn't even have had bus fare to get home. And now I owed three thousand dollars to a bookie, with thirty percent interest compounded daily. I added it up in my head and realized that in a week, assuming he let it go that far, I would owe him almost nineteen thousand dollars."

"Odd, that's about what you won in the first place." Dee sat up, scooted to the far end of the couch, and put her stockinged feet in my lap. I automatically began rubbing the arch of her left foot. She closed her eyes and emitted a feline purr.

"I walked out into the dark night in a daze. I never even noticed the fellow until we had smacked into each other at full stride. I would have gone down like he did, but I had a good fifty pounds on him, and I don't weigh more than 175. As I reached down to help him up, I apprehended that I recognized his face, but I failed to recall from where. I doubted he was a student, but I felt as if I knew him from school somehow. When he smiled up at me and called me by name, I realized I had seen him on the sideline at football games. His name was Sheldon Cooper and he was friends with a coach or a trainer or some such, though I was of the impression he had nothing officially to do with the program.

"He invited me back into the bar and bought me a beer. Several beers actually, followed by rather too many shots of Jim Beam. I'm unclear on how long we sat there, but this gent just had a way about him that made me feel comfortable, like I could tell him anything. It wasn't that he was handsome or anything of that sort. Whether he was an extraordinary listener or I just needed to unburden myself, I'm not sure, but I told him the whole story. And he continued buying drinks. I vaguely remember him eventually helping me to his car and giving me a ride home. As he assisted me to my door, he said something or other about my having nothing to worry about, that he was going to fix everything. I had no idea what it was at the time, but he slipped something into the pocket of my jacket.

"The next morning, I woke up to the first hangover of my life. I had never been much of a drinker and the night before was an absolute record for me. Thankfully, it was Sunday and I would not have to worry about classes until the next morning. Lilith was out of the house by the time I awakened, so I just lay in bed for a time waiting for my head to explode and be done with it. Besides, I was fairly sure I would upchuck if I tried to get up. After maybe twenty or thirty minutes, I sat up on the side of the bed with my head in my hands and my eyes closed against the late-morning sun streaming through the window until I felt steady enough to try getting up. It was only after I got to my feet that I realized I had slept in my clothes—coat, shoes and all. I was in no shape to care, though, so I staggered out the door to the toilet and then to the kitchen, where I found some Alka-Seltzer in the cabinet. I managed to keep that down and sat at the kitchen table waiting for it to quiet the brass band that had replaced the gongs in my cranium."

"Takes a while." I remembered the one time I had overindulged in college. The hangover had been what got me to cut way back. He turned back toward us when I spoke but didn't come away from the door, but leaned on the facing, his arms crossed.

"Eventually, I felt well enough to put some water on for tea and make some dry toast. I most certainly did not feel like eating, but I was hoping the bread would absorb some of the bile in my stomach. I have no idea if that actually works, but that's what my meemaw taught me, so I've always done it. A cup of chamomile tea and two slices of toast later, I was feeling almost human, so I walked somewhat more steadily back to the bedroom to get into some pajamas and robe. It was when I removed my jacket that the note fell out of the pocket. It took a few moments, but the memory Cooper putting it there floated to the surface of my still half-pickled brain. Retrieving it from the floor nearly made me black out and it took me at least thirty seconds to focus my eyes sufficiently to read it, but I at last figured out it said 'Entrance to M. Weinberg Garden, Monday, Noon.'"

"The Marjorie Weinberg Garden?" I asked as I switched to her right foot and got another purr. "I've seen it on the Internet, but never in person. Beautiful."

He nodded tersely. "I slept a great deal of that day away but still felt rather unpleasant the next say, so I cancelled all my morning classes. At 11:55, I stood rather unsteadily at the entrance. Cooper appeared perhaps a minute or two later. He smiled and handed me a Starbuck's cup. I smelled it—hazelnut. How he knew that was my favorite, I didn't know, but I took a long sip and felt the warmth course through me. We made some small talk for a minute, about the weather; about the basketball team; oddly enough, about his favorite authors, John Steinbeck and Robert B. Parker, two authors I also quite enjoy. Finally, I asked him why we were there. His little mole mouth curled around his yellow pointy teeth into a grin and he told me we were going to solve each other's problems. I asked him what problem he had with which I could possibly help. His smile widened and he informed me that he worked for the bookmaker to whom I was indebted. Well, his language was somewhat more colorful than that—it involved my testicles—but you get the idea."

"Aha," I said.

"Aha?" Dee asked.

"Yes, aha. It seemed significant, or at least seemed like it should seem significant, but I was unable to figure out exactly how. So I finally asked what that meant for me. He said that, as a professor at the school, I was in a unique position to help his boss with some projects. That was the exact word he used—projects. After taking a few long draws from his coffee and an even longer draw from an odoriferous unfiltered cigarette, he again smiled and explained that I had some students in my classes who participated in various school sports. I nodded because that was the best I could do at the moment. I did, in fact, have two starters on the men's basketball team, as well as starters and important bench players on the women's team. I taught some foundation level classes that are required for nearly all majors and, for some reason, I became popular with the athletic department, which meant that, at any given time, I was likely to have several varsity athletes in my classes. I was starting to get quite a dreadful feeling about what he was telling me. Then he said that, as their professor, I had the ability to do things to either assure their eligibility or lack thereof for any given game. I immediately apprehended half of his implication, but was unclear why he would want me ever to do something to keep someone from playing in a game."

"Why would he?" asked Dee.

"Alter the betting line," I said. "Change the outcome or the margin of victory."

"But keeping players out was bad for Northwestern, right?"

"It didn't make sense to me either, until I realized it didn't matter to this miscreant if Northwestern won, only that he had an inside track to knowing who would win and/or by how much they were likely to win or lose. But either way, it hardly mattered, because I was ready to take the knee-breaking or even a bullet to the back of my skull rather than allow myself to be a part of rigging games or cheating of any kind. My rules, you know. And I told this man as much.

"He said he knew all about my rules and he also knew that there were certain rules that took precedence over other rules, the most important of which is something to the effect of protect the women and children first. Puzzled, I had no choice but to assent. He reached into his jacket pocket to retrieve a rather large cell phone. He tapped on the screen a few times, paused, and turned the screen toward me. It was video of my bookmaker, a man named Jonas Cobb, walking toward the entrance to the bakery Lilith and I frequented, the Alliance Bakery. As he started toward the door, it opened. I'm not sure how I remained upright, because all the blood left my face and upper extremities as I watched Cobb barrel headlong into—into Lilith."

Chapter 23

Knowing Tuttle as I do, I was sure they would have to use his family's safety for leverage against him. He would never, even as despoiled as he had clearly become, do something that dishonest, even if his life depended on it. And someone willing to rig college sporting events to gain an advantage in betting on it wouldn't think twice about using that perceived weakness against him.

"What exactly did they make you do?" asked Dee. She stood and stretched her legs then flopped back onto the couch and put her head back on my lap. It was well past 2:00 a.m.

"Well, the keeping them in the games part was a relatively simple and predicable proposition. If a student was struggling, which was somewhat rare, considering the rigorous academic standards for everyone, including athletes at NU, my job was simply to fudge a grade here and there or let someone turn in a paper late with no penalty. Whatever was needed to bump the grade to maintain eligibility."

"Did you just have to help all athletes?" I started to run my fingers through her hair, to which she responded by nuzzling deeper into the couch. Soon her breathing became slow and regular.

"No." Tuttle yawned and walked back to the table, dropping heavily into a chair. He rubbed his bloodshot eyes, stretched and then winced, as if the motion hurt. He rubbed his left lower back. "Only when I was contacted by Cooper. I would get a text with the student's name and I knew what to do. I was only required to help a few students. I went entire semesters without hearing from him. But when it was time, I was to work quickly because the student's situation was apparently dire and his or her participation in the game was apparently vital to the betting line."

"So what about if they didn't want someone to play?" I asked.

"That was somewhat trickier. The suggestion was to "lose" a paper or test or accuse a student of academic dishonesty of some kind. Surprisingly, I was asked to do this at least once every semester. Never to the same student, but always to a starting player."

"How long did this go on?" I asked.

"Six semesters, so roughly two-and-a-half years. They did fix my problem and more. My assistance must have been highly beneficial to them, because they not only wiped out my debt to them, but also paid off all our debts, including replenishing all our investments. It was many hundreds of thousands of dollars. Additionally, an envelope appeared in my faculty mailbox at the end of each semester containing ten thousand dollars. If it weren't for the fact that it was eating my soul bit-by-bit, it would have actually been a good life."

"Why not go to the police?" Dee's eyes were still closed. She had been awake the whole time.

"Lilith. And even if I told her everything and we left, where could we be safe? Also, they showed me videos of Cobb knocking on my parents' door dressed as a utility worker. He asked to come in to check something to do with their electric outlets. They never suspected they had let a cold-blooded killer into their home.

"What changed?" I asked.

"It was two years ago May, the last day of the semester, when Cooper texted me that I was to meet him at the same place as our first meeting, the Marjorie Weinberg Garden, the next day at noon. Cooper was standing there when I arrived. As on our first meeting, he greeted me with a cup of Starbuck's hazelnut coffee. He told me that his boss was quite happy with me and that I was getting the call to the big leagues.

"There are leagues?" Dee sat up and tousled her hair with both hands.

"There are definitely strata. He handed me a business card with only an address in North Shore on Locust Road. On the back were written the next day's date and 11:00 a.m."

"Locust Road is high rent, if I'm not mistaken," I said.

"You have no idea. I marveled as the houses grew ever more opulent, but I simply could not conceive of what awaited me when I arrived. The drive went on forever and ended in a circle, which surrounded a grand fountain. The white marble two-story house looked like a French villa and seemed as long as a football field. Columns lined the front of the house, holding up the balcony, which ran from end to end. A butler greeted me as the taxi pulled away. He led me inside and past two huge spiral staircases to a veranda that overlooked a lawn on which Comiskey Park could have fit. Sitting on the veranda was a man I would have guessed to be 45, though I have since found he was in excess of 60 at that time. He was dressed

in black silk pajamas, black slippers, and a black silk robe with eyes

and hair exactly the same shade. He introduced himself as Merton

Bell and politely asked me to sit and have some lemonade with him.

It was a warm day and I didn't want to make this man angry, so I

had lemonade. I hate lemonade."

"Johnny," I said, "'more matter with less art.'"

"Oh, yes, it is getting rather late, isn't it? Well, long story

somewhat shorter, this man was the boss of Cooper's boss. His son

was, in his words, a slightly imbecilic young man who had, through

Bell's influence, gotten into Northwestern, where he was, to put it

mildly, floundering. Bell wanted me to quit my job, move in with

him and become his son's full-time tutor and babysitter. I asked why

he didn't just get his son's grades fixed. His answer shocked me. He

said he wanted more for his son than the life of a thug, even a rich

one, and knew he would need to actually learn something in college

rather than be handed his sheepskin after four years of dissipation

and debauchery. Those were the exact words he used."

"A thug with aspirations, even if for his son, is refreshing in a

twisted way." Dee scooted against me, raised my arm above her head and laid her head against my chest. I wrapped my arm around her, hugging her and rubbing her upper arm.

"I reminded him I was married, to which he replied that Lilith—he called her by name—was more than welcome as well. He even told me not to worry; she need never know that there was anything shady, as he never did any real business at home, reserving that for his office downtown, preferring never to mix family with work. For all she had to know, I would be employed by a man who had made his billions the old fashioned way—through inheritance. So I put in my resignation and we moved in with Bell and his wife and son and all their other servants. I worked with his son every day, soliciting help from some former colleagues in other departments when I was over my head. I actually enjoyed the time and the young man was, though clearly not Northwestern material, not as dimwitted as his father had led me to believe. And his grades actually did improve—quite a lot, actually."

"But then?" I really needed him to kick it in gear.

"Everything was fine until my conscience overcame me and I decided that I couldn't lie to Lilith anymore. So I sat her down and came clean. Told her everything. She didn't believe me. Said I was being paranoid or trying to play a sick joke on her. I had hoped she would be so appalled that she would want to run away. We could do that now since my parents had both passed on. It was just the two of us, but she was too happy where we were and acted as if I was insane any time I talked about it, so I had to come up with some other way to get out this mess."

"And the other way was to send someone to zip me?"

"Well, one day your name just popped into my head. I thought if anybody could help me it was you, but calling you up wasn't really an option in my mind. Too much chance of them finding out; they monitored all my communications and you have a bit if a reputation. I didn't want to get you killed trying to come to our rescue. So I came up with a story of a past dalliance between you and Lilith and requested they put a hit on you."

"Do you know how close I came on at least two occasions to dying, not to mention nearly losing Deanna? And that it was only by mere happenstance that I even knew you were connected with it?"

"I told Rutger to tell you it was me that was after you, but he apparently waited too long. I'm deeply sorry. But I was at the end of my tether, and I simply couldn't think of another way to get you to come after me. I hoped you would either suspect I was in trouble or at least come after me to stop the attempts on your life. Please believe me that Deanna's kidnapping was neither authorized nor requested by me. It was Bernhard who did that on his own. I guess he knew of your prowess from previous confrontations he and his lack-pate brother had had with you, along with the fact that you had managed to neutralize so many of Bell's men, and he deduced something that I had overlooked, which was that you would back down if it meant protecting Deanna. So he proposed the agreement to keep you from continuing to come after me, which is exactly what I wanted, but I could hardly tell him that. I see now it was a harebrained scheme, but I didn't know where else to turn."

"Okay, one possibly unrelated question," I said, "When I was in Chicago, I found a dead guy in your fridge. Name was Bloom, I think."

"Milo Bloom. Didn't know he was dead, but no one liked him. I overheard Bell say one day that he needed to, and I quote, 'keep his fat mouth shut and keep it in his pants.'"

My brain hurt; if I weren't wasted by fatigue, I would be angry, but all I felt was enervation.

"I'm sure I'll have questions tomorrow, but I'm finished."

Rousing my lovely sleepy-headed wife from my lap, I went into the bedroom and got Johnny a sheet, blanket, and pillow for the couch. Dee followed me into the bedroom, but didn't come back out. By the time I got back, her breathing told me she was sleeping deeply. It took me nearly thirty seconds to be in the land of Morpheus with her.

Chapter 24

I had a dream that we were in Chicago and Merton Bell was chasing us. Only I didn't know what he looked like, so in my dream he looked like Al Capone. And his head was huge, like the pilgrim balloons in the Macy's Parade. For reasons that completely escape me, Mandy Patinkin, as Inigo Montoya from *The Princess Bride*, was with us. He kept shouting that Bell had killed his father and should prepare to die. Bell was shooting at us with his finger, but it shot real bullets. I was running from him; however, it was like my body was partially paralyzed and I could barely move. This would not seem to be as much of a problem as it could have been since the bullets Bell was shooting at me were moving in ultra-slow-motion as well. Nonetheless, two were coming at me, one at each eye, and were about to hit me in the face. Oddly, one smelled like coffee and the other bacon. I tried to scream but nothing came out; I woke up just as the bullets were about to make impact. Phew—too close for comfort. I picked up my phone and checked the time—9:15AM.

I realized the reason Bell's bullets smelled like they did, as the rich aromas of freshly brewed coffee and frying bacon were wafting in from the kitchen. I assumed it was Dee's doing, but I rolled over to find her still dead asleep beside me. Couldn't be Eddie since we left him at my parents' house. And besides, he knows he's not allowed to use the stove since the sautéed kibble incident of 2010. That only left Johnny Tuttle.

The sun shone brilliantly outside, indicating that the storm had passed. I squinted out the window to find that the street was still covered in at least two feet of snow with two barely discernible ruts in each lane made by what appeared to be a large-wheeled vehicle, a 4x4 truck, no doubt. There was no indication of the city having been through to clear it—somewhat surprising on the day after Thanksgiving. I guess Black Friday would have to wait until the roads cleared. Aside from birds in the trees, the only movement I saw was Ralph Parker shoveling his driveway a few doors up.

The delicious smells of breakfast became even more pronounced as I opened the door. I espied Tuttle flipping a pancake at the stove. His back was too me, so I tried to make some noise so as not to frighten him. One should never surprise anyone standing in front of a pan of frying pig fat.

"I love pancakes, especially when I don't have to cook—"

My sentence was interrupted by the unmistakable ringing click of a gun hammer being pulled back.

"Harry Shalan I presume." The thick German accent and voice left no question as to their owner.

Bernhard Stultz was like a slightly larger, slightly better looking version of his brother Rutger. Though he was sitting, I guessed him to be a shade taller than I, about six feet three inches or so. He was not a huge man, though his arms showed the development of a man who did actual physical labor rather than that of a weight lifter. His hair, a shade darker than blonde but a shade lighter than brown, was close cropped though not in what one would call a buzz cut. His face was handsome in a craggy way, like someone who spends a lot of time outside. Crow's feet were only beginning to develop around his ice blue eyes, undoubtedly his most striking feature. The only things that marred his face, or some would say gave it even more character, were a small amount of scar tissue around the edges of his eyes and a nose that, though it probably started out fine-looking and straight, was now as crooked as Eddie's hind leg. He had been in some fights in his life. His teeth were straight and white and surrounded by darkish lips that were not quite too thick, though they bordered on it. He reminded me of Robert Shaw in his younger days, like when he was the villain in one of the James Bond films. *From Russia With Love*? Not sure. Anyway, not the old grizzled Captain Quint from *Jaws*, but from when he was still hard, steely-eyed, and anvil-jawed. He had what could only be described as a friendly smile on his face.

"How's your brother? He recover or is he still trying to shoot people with his finger?"

"Rutger was never the brighter of the two of us, but your neighbor's blow to his skull did not help the matter. He has been forced into retirement, leaving the family business to me."

"Well, I'm sure you're more than up to the task." I leaned my back against the wall at the end of the couch with my arms crossed. Shalan—always casual, even with a gun pointed at his face. I was conscious not to flex my biceps. Didn't want to make Stultz feel so inferior that he would drop the gun and run away screaming. It just didn't seem sporting.

"Yes, well, it makes for a busy life. But one does what one has to."

"Breakfast is ready." Tuttle placed a steaming plate of pancakes on the table.

"Ah, good, I am famished. May I have your word that we can eat in peace with no attempts at bravery?"

"I'm too hungry to try anything, trust me. Mind if I go get my wife? You probably remember her from when you kidnapped her."

"Ah, good times. Please, our meal would not be the same without her lovely face and cheerful company."

I stepped away from the wall and walked to the bedroom, sitting on Dee's side of the bed and playing lightly with her tousled auburn hair. She smiled sleepily.

"Hi dollface. Is that breakfast I smell?"

"Yes, pancakes, eggs, bacon, and a side of Stultz."

"Huh?" She sat bolt upright.

"Don't panic, but Bernhard Stultz is out there."

"Is Johnny okay?"

"He's fine. Stultz is being ineffably civilized. Quite nice for a professional thug, really."

She gave me a sour look as she got up and tottered to the bathroom. In a record never approached before or since, she was out in her pink fuzzy robe and slippers and her hair up in a ponytail in under two minutes. Even just a few minutes out of bed with no makeup on, she still made my heart feel wiggly.

"Ah, Mrs. Shalan," Stultz said when we came through the door into the great room, "what a delight to see you again. I'm terribly sorry to intrude."

"G'morning Mr. Stultz," said Dee sleepily but agreeably as Stultz rose, took her right hand in his and kissed it lightly. "Please, don't worry your handsome little head about it. After all, unlike last time, I have the advantage."

I realized at that moment for the first time just how unflappable my wife is. A man who had, at least in part, been responsible for one of the most traumatic events of her life was standing in our home pointing a gun at her, and she was exchanging pleasantries with him like he was an old friend.

"How exactly do you come to this conclusion, liebchen? I believe you will agree that I am the only armed person here."

Yes, there's that," said Dee pleasantly, looking my way, "but you don't have the most dangerous weapon in the room. That would belong to me through marriage."

Stultz smiled. I could tell he was genuinely fond of her and, oddly enough, I got the impression that she actually felt affection toward him. Maybe it was the way he had treated her in Cleveland, or maybe they were just simpatico. Either way, it was to our advantage for him to like her. It could give us as an edge if things degenerated into a fire fight, which I certainly hoped they wouldn't.

"So," I finally said, "the pancakes aren't getting any warmer. How about we eat while we talk?"

And that we did. Stultz holstered his gun, though he did insist that Dee sit next to him and I sit opposite him at our square table. Maybe I would have to shoot this guy just on principle.

Plates and mugs filled and the first hungry bites swallowed, I decided to break the ice.

"So what's the plan here?"

"The plan, mein freund, is to take Herr Tuttle back to Chicago, and leave his fate in the hands of our employer."

"You are aware, I assume, that my plan would be somewhat different from that."

"Your plan, I presume, would be somewhat diametrically opposed to my plan."

"Somewhat."

"That leaves us at a bit of an impasse."

"How do we overcome that civilly?"

"You scrap your plan, hand Herr Tuttle over. Quite civil."

"Counterproposal—call off your men and let us go."

"That is a lovely proposal, but I have promised that I would return this gentleman to Bell. As is true of you, my word is my bond. What have we without our integrity?"

"There are no circumstances that override your word to your boss? What's the most integrated thing to do—keep your word or do what's right?"

"Right, wrong, who's to say? Do what you say you will do—this is black and white. Right and wrong are messy. I am employed by Merton Bell. If he says to do a thing, I do this thing. And, in exchange, he remunerates me quite generously."

"Bell told you to protect Dee after you kidnapped her?"

"I do improvise when I see fit, true."

"Listen to Johnny's story and then see how you feel."

"Very well. I am in no hurry. But do not expect me to change my mind."

"Johnny, tell him."

He did. Though it was an abridged version of the one he told the night before, he hit the important parts. At first, Stultz listened impassively as he ate, but his expression changed subtly. The time between bites grew longer and longer as Stultz became more and more absorbed by Tuttle's depiction of his apparently impregnable prison. I imagined that the absolute best I could hope for would be for Stultz to let us go and make up a story to tell Bell. A long shot to be sure, but, like the ant trying to move the rubber tree plant, I had high hopes.

Tuttle added the ending we hadn't heard last night, in which he and Lilith went out one day to the movies and, against Lilith's rather vehement opposition, just never went back. They left everything behind, got on the interstate, and just drove to Parkersburg, stopping only long enough to charge new clothes and toiletries at a mall. I figured that was how they tracked them in this direction. How they caught up with them here was somewhat more mysterious.

"But where's Lilith now?" asked Dee, rising with me to clear the table while I made another pot of coffee.

"I'm not saying. You can pull my fingernails out Bernhard. But you can't have Lilith."

"Johnny, you have my solemn word that no harm will come to Lilith."

Tuttle looked at Stultz, obviously irresolute about whether to trust him.

"Johnny, Stultz is good for his word. He'll kill you if he has to, but if he promises you that he won't hurt your wife, you can take his promise as readily as you would mine."

"I put her up at a hotel off the interstate across the Ohio near Marietta. Let's just leave it at that."

"So," I said, turning to Stultz, "what do you think?

"I think this man went out of his head for a short period of time and has been paying for that indiscretion for a long, long time.

"Too long if you ask me Bernhard," said Dee. Bernhard. Why did Bernhard have to be so ruggedly handsome? If I weren't so self-assured, I might be jealous.

"But what of it? Is this not life? We do things for which there are consequences, both good and bad. Is it not he who put his wife in danger with his reckless behavior? I am simply the piper to whom he must pay."

"But pay what?" I asked. "Does he owe a life sentence for a few months insanity?"

Stultz stretched and rubbed his rough hand across the coarse two-day growth of whiskers on his jaw. An occasional white hair was mixed in with his dark sandy brown facial hair. He then got up from the table and walked across the room to the back door, which looked out over the back yard. After standing sphinxlike, staring out the window into the snowy wonderland for a few minutes, he shook his head quickly and waved his right hand back and forth in front of his face, like he was trying to rid himself of a fly.

"Very well." He spoke without turning to us. "What is your proposal?"

Chapter 25

Stultz made a couple phone calls and then we talked. It was nearly noon by the time our plan, such as it was, was complete. Dee and I would take Tuttle, collect Lilith, and hit the road fast for parts unknown, trading our phones for a couple new, hopefully untraceable ones. Stultz would explain the situation to Bell and either convince him that Tuttle would never go to the police and would live under my protection and everything would be okay or we would be looking over our shoulders for the foreseeable future and Stultz would be persona non grata—at best.

He already had our cell numbers in his contacts from the Cleveland incident, but those were going to change soon, so he gave me his cell number and stepped out into the dazzling afternoon sun, which had already started melting the snow. Our landlord had cleared our walk and the roads had been plowed. I watched through our bedroom window as Stultz stepped carefully through the slush on the side of the street to the passenger seat of a black Mercedes SUV parked three doors up the street. They must have been there all night because I could see where they had been dug out. Hard to tell where the passengers had stayed. Maybe in there. Not very comfortable, but I knew from the stakeouts I've been on that comfort is not always a primary concern.

After a few minutes, the SUV and its twin from another few spots down and on the other side of the street started up and carefully pulled away. A half block down, Stultz' vehicle cut across at an intersection, u-turned to the other side of the boulevard and, along with the second vehicle, headed, I assumed, toward the interstate to begin the trip back to Chicago.

When I got back out to the great room, Dee had finished cleaning up from breakfast and was on the phone, probably with her parents. Tuttle was in the bathroom, but the door was ajar and I could hear he was also on the phone. Nothing else for me to do, so I pulled out my cell to call my folks and catch them up as much as I safely could and make sure it was okay to leave Eddie with them for a while.

"Is this fella' Tuttle in a lot of trouble?" asked my father.

"A lot doesn't quite cover it."

"Well," said my mother from another extension, "he's in good hands with the two of you."

"I hope so Mom. I'll be in touch occasionally to let you know we're okay. You won't be able to reach our cells anymore, but you'll know we're still alive."

"That's the important thing, honey. You tell Dee to keep my baby safe."

"Oh—I almost forgot. Dee and I ended up abandoning the Escape down at the bottom of your hill. If I leave the keys in our mailbox, can you come move it? Hate to leave it out there not knowing how long we'll be gone."

"Now Harry, don't drive crazy," said Mom with more than a hint of worry in her voice. It always seemed funny to me that I carry a gun and sometimes get in scrapes with people who want to harm or kill me, but the scariest part of my job to my mom is my fast car.

Dee had already started, so I packed. I always had a travel case ready in case I needed to go somewhere hastily. It contained a shaving kit, clean underwear, socks, a couple of days' changes of clothes, a couple sets of workout clothes that could double as pajamas, an extra wall charger for my cell, an extra gun, ammunition for it and my primary weapon, a gun cleaning kit, and $5,000 in cash. The money turned out to be invaluable in this case because we weren't going to be able to use credit cards for fear they could be traced. The case was large enough for another week's worth of clothing, which I added. My laptop and Kindle were already packed in their case, so I was ready to go in about ten minutes.

While Dee finished packing, Tuttle and I went downstairs to dig Ellie out. At the bottom of the stairs, we found the two brooms from the night before, along with a snow shovel. I took the shovel, Tuttle both brooms.

The snow was heavy and wet. Tuttle and I took turns with the shovel, and once we had a path all the way around, we started in on the pile on top.

"Will it work?" Tuttle used the push broom to clear the roof, front windshield, and hood.

"Stultz' plan?" I dug off the back window and trunk. "I wish I could say. I believe Stultz will do what he says he will."

"If Bell says no?"

"We make him say yes."

"How's that?"

"I'll let you know when I figure it out." I said with a smile as I finished the back bumper and taillights.

"Did you know Stultz would go for it?" He re-cleared the path we had filled in with the snow from the car.

"Not for sure, but I believed that he might."

"Do you know Stultz that well?"

"Not personally, but I know he does what he says he'll do and, despite his protestations, right and wrong do mean something to him. Especially with people like you who are not a part of his world by choice. He would feel free to be as savage as he needs to be with me or even with Dee. But you're no more a thug than I'm a ballet dancer."

Car cleaned, we headed upstairs. Dee was nearly finished, so I hauled what I could to the car. By the time I had trudged back up to our third floor apartment, she was packed and ready, so we all three made our way down to the Mustang, which I had started before I came up the last time. On my way past, I dropped the keys to our Escape into our mailbox for my dad. It was already relatively toasty when we got in because the temperature had risen to the low 40s and also the snow had insulated it quite well. Tuttle insisted on taking the back seat despite a brief, halfhearted argument from Dee. I had to finesse it a little to get it off the slick snow around the wheels, but once I got out onto the street, it was just wet pavement. I took the same U-turn Stultz' vehicle had and headed off to get Lilith Tuttle. Dee waved forlornly at our apartment as we passed.

"Bye."

I took her hand in mine and gave it a squeeze. "We'll be back soon babydoll, I promise."

Chapter 26

The freak storm turned out to be freaky on a couple of levels. When we hit Interstate 77 going south, the snow grew shallower and shallower until there was just a dusting left on the sides of mountains. By the time we hit Ripley, often the snowiest spot between Parkersburg and Charleston, Ellie's readout told me that the outside temperature was 53 degrees and there was no indication there had been snow at all the night before.

We had picked up Lilith, who was checked out of the hotel and waiting in the lobby with all of Johnny's and her luggage when we pulled up. After clearing off the Tuttles' car and leaving the hotel, we stopped at Wal-Mart to get burn phones and got them activated. I also picked up a pair of walkie-talkies and spare batteries for each. I gave Tuttle one on the way out to our cars. By the time we hit the interstate, it was still only 3:00PM, so we wasted no time heading south.

By supper time, we were between Charleston and Huntington. The Tuttles walkie-talkied that they wanted pizza, so we stopped at the first Gino's we saw, which happened to be in Cross

Lanes. We passed a Pizza Hut, but Gino's is a local chain that we had eaten in before and liked. Being 5:30 and a Friday and a holiday weekend, it was pretty slammed, but we only waited about fifteen minutes to get a table. Everyone was hungry, so the conversation to start was centered on our order, which turned out to be a large veggie, a large Hawaiian, and sweet teas all around.

The order out of the way and drinks delivered, there was a slight awkward lull in the conversation. There was obvious tension between Lilith and Johnny, but I put it off to stress. I excused myself to find the little boys' room. Upon my return, as I approached the table, Dee gave me a desperate look in response to which I slowed down and raised my eyebrows. She subtly nodded her head toward Johnny and Lilith, who were locked in a heated, albeit quiet, conversation. I stepped to the table and took my seat.

"Not happy with the order, folks? We can call Tammy back and switch if you just can't stand the idea of pineapple on your pizza."

"Harry," said Johnny quietly through pursed lips, his face down so as not to draw attention, "explain to Lilith, please, that returning to Chicago is simply not an option."

"I've spent time with Merton," said Lilith, just as vehemently and just as quietly as Johnny, "and I simply refuse to believe that, if we just explain how desperate we are to leave, he would not let us go. He has never been anything but polite to me."

"I'm sure he has, Lilith," I said, "but please, never mistake polite for compassionate. He's polite to you simply because it's good for business to be polite to people in the outside world. And for all he knew, you saw him as a fine, upstanding citizen, an image that serves him well. But the real Merton Bell would slit your throat without a moment's hesitation if it served his purposes. He runs gambling, drugs, prostitution, racketeering, and at least a dozen other terrible, illegal activities in a large portion of Chicago, one of the toughest cities in the world. He can't keep his seat of power without being a murderous man without the slightest compunction about doing away with whatever—or whoever—he needs to."

"How do you know so much? You don't even know Merton." She always called him by his first name. Something bothered me about that, but I couldn't place what.

"No, but I've met his kind many times. Some may be more or less drawn to the violence that accompanies their business, but none will live long if they don't quickly learn to embrace it. The underworld is a lot like a shark tank. One drop of blood and you're chum before you even realize what happened. Merton Bell is a shark among sharks."

"Then why are we even bothering to hope that Stultz can succeed?" asked Johnny, wide-eyed.

"Well, first," said Dee, "Stultz is a pretty big shark himself and can explain to him more effectively that it's simply not worth the trouble to chase down a guppy like you, especially when you're being guarded by the only man who may be tougher than he is."

"May be?"

"Drop it. And second Stultz can handle himself in a tough spot. You go and Bell will put a bullet through your brain without you even realizing he has a gun."

Again, Dee surprised me with how readily she had adapted to this thug life. She analyzed the situation perfectly, despite our not having discussed it in any depth until then.

"And third," I added, "we aren't counting on Stultz. Every hour that we're moving away in a direction they could only guess before Stultz even gets to Bell is another hour between us and danger."

"Are you tougher?" asked Lilith.

"No idea. Ultimately, it's a meaningless question. I'm good, but there's always somebody better. I don't spend a lot of time thinking about it. I'm here and I'm willing, so I'll have to do."

At that point, Tammy, our perky little waitress, who was no more than five feet tall with white blonde hair, came to refill our drinks. She wore a Nitro Wildcats ribbon beside her name tag. In our initial conversation, we found she was a cheerleader and that everyone in town was quite excited for the playoff game the next day at Laidley Field. As she moved around the table, I asked who they were playing, though I knew myself they were playing Martinsburg.

"I don't know." Tammy had the charming southern West Virginia twang. "Martinsburg, maybe? I just cheer. Don't really watch the games."

"Well, I'm sure you do a great job, sweetie," said Dee, patting her on the upper arm as she filled her tea.

"Y'all should come to the game," said Tammy. "It's supposed to be a close one. That's what my boyfriend says anyway."

"We'd love to," I said, "but sadly, we'll be far away from here by that time."

"Where y'all headed?" she asked.

"Well, I'd tell you, but then I'd just have to kill you," I said with a wide grin.

"Uh-oh," Tammy shouted with a laugh, "wouldn't want that, would I?"

Lilith looked troubled, but protested no further after Tammy left. The conversation turned to idle chatter, in which Lilith did not participate, until the pizzas arrived, by which time she began talking quietly with Dee. Crisis seemingly averted, we enjoyed our feast. I left a 25% tip for Tammy.

"Good luck tomorrow, sweetheart!" said Dee to Tammy as we walked toward the exit.

"Thanks," she said with a toothy grin, "have a safe trip to wherever!"

It was pitch dark, which made it feel like the middle of the night, though it was only 7:00PM as we walked out of the restaurant to our cars. I took the lead as we drove back through Cross Lanes to I-64 and headed west. Dee could sleep in a car like no one else I know and was out in less than five minutes. Passing Huntington and several small towns in West Virginia, we crossed the border into Kentucky by a little before 8:00PM. The highway was nearly deserted, so I set my cruise control on 75. Didn't want to waste time, but also didn't want to leave a record we had been there by getting a ticket.

To alleviate the boredom as I drove, I watched for houses lit up early with Christmas lights. By the time we got to Lexington, where we would be heading south, I was starting to see double, so we pulled into a Ramada about 9:45. Paying cash, with a little extra to the desk clerk not to show ID and not to be remembered if anyone asked, we got two adjoining non-smoking rooms.

By 10:15, Dee and I had our teeth brushed, our jammies on, and were in bed. It had been a long day, so I wasn't expecting it to work, but I nuzzled up to her neck and began nibbling on her ear. To my slight surprise, she rolled into me, pitched her left leg over my hip, and pulled me close.

I guess she wasn't that tired.

Chapter 27

The day dawned dazzlingly bright, beautiful, and unseasonably warm, though it was still dark when my alarm went off at 6:00AM. Using the light from my phone and working as quietly as I could, though I have no idea why, since Dee could sleep through Armageddon, I dug through my bag to find some sweats, socks, and my running shoes, then made one of the small pots of coffee in the room and headed out the door. There was a little country road outside the hotel called Judy Lane that the desk clerk, a petite young brunette woman of about 25 or so with perfect teeth and face to match, told me was a decent place to run, so I headed out. I'm not sure how far I ran before I turned around, though I would guess based on experience that it was just about 3-1/2 miles. The temperature was in the Goldilocks zone—not too hot, not too cold, but just right. It was warm enough that I worked up a good sweat without getting overheated. As I ran, the sky lightened up progressively, allowing me to see the lovely rolling hills of the outskirts of Lexington. I passed several horse farms with countless sleek, powerful looking thoroughbreds munching peacefully on grass in fields next to the road. One young colt, probably a late spring foal, ran alongside me for a bit. It was a splendid sorrel with a white blaze on its nose and white markings on its lower legs, known by horsey people as boots or socks, depending on who you ask. It jogged with me for a few hundred yards before it decided I was too slow to be any fun and peeled away, with what I took to be a condescending snort, to find a faster playmate.

"Showoff." I don't think it heard me because it just kept running.

There was minimal traffic, which was good, because the shoulder was pretty much nonexistent, but that was really the closest thing there was to a negative on the whole run. It was one of those times that all runners have experienced (though not as often as we would like) where all was right with the world. My legs felt good, my lungs felt expansive, and my brain was clear. I felt like I could run all day.

I was at a relatively slow, comfortable pace to start, which, for me, usually translated into about a nine-minute mile. I could have talked comfortably, but since I was alone, I decided against it. I felt strong and loose when I turned back at the thirty minute mark, so I kicked my pace up a notch and steadily raised my turnover rate until I was at the top of my range as I neared the hotel. No one passed by, but they probably wouldn't have seen me if they had, because I'm pretty sure I was approaching the speed of light. I was happy to arrive at the hotel in just under 25 minutes. Okay, maybe I was closer to the speed of sound instead. Negative splits—the breakfast of champions.

Dee was already up and in the shower when I hobbled into the room. I was still sweating way too much to shower, so I bypassed the chance to join her and sat on the edge of an armchair with my shirt off drinking most of the quart bottle of water I'd bought at our last gas stop the night before. I had turned on the TV and was watching SportsCenter with the volume up pretty high to overcome the furnace blower, so I didn't hear Dee come out of the shower.

"Hi sweaty boy," she said from just outside the bathroom door, wearing nothing but her patented naughty grin.

"Hi to you, nudie girl," I replied. "I love your outfit."

She sashayed across the room, making sure to give her hips some extra swing, leaned down to kiss me, and then went to get dressed. I gave her perfect bum a playful smack as she walked away, to which she responded with a giggle. I had finally cooled off enough to want a cup of coffee, so I poured one for me and one for Dee, which I handed to her on one of her passes between the bathroom and the bed. Whenever I watched her get ready, I was reminded of why she didn't need to run to stay so svelte. She had to do a thousand laps across the room just to get into a pair of panties and a bra and brush her hair. I knew I still had plenty of time to shower and be dressed and packed before she was, so I relaxed into my chair and enjoyed my favorite spectator sport—my stunning wife preparing for the day.

With my coffee gone, my wife fully clothed, and SportsCenter starting over, I decided it was time to hit the shower. I was in and out, shaved, dressed, and packed in twenty minutes, leaving me at least another twenty to wait until Dee was ready, so I called the Tuttles. Lilith answered and told me Johnny was in the shower and that they would be ready in about a half hour.

"Gonna go get some more coffee," I said. "You want another?"

"No, thanks Honey," she replied, "but will you see if you can get me a Diet Coke?"

"One Diet Coke, check"

I took the elevator down to the lobby—my legs were still a bit wobbly for the steps—and followed the signs to the in-house restaurant. As soon as I set foot in the door, the greeter met me with a shy smile. She was probably my age with red hair, though not red like Dee's red. This woman's was more strawberry blonde. She was tall and waifishly thin with long, slender fingers. I wondered if she played the piano. When she asked me if I wanted a table, I saw why she smiled with her mouth closed. Her front teeth were quite crooked. It obviously bothered her, which was a shame, because she really did have a lovely face.

"Actually, I was hoping for just a large black coffee and a bottle of Diet Coke to go."

She disappeared with a friendly nod and was replaced a minute later by a short round waitress in a brown dress under a brown and white checkered apron and sensible white walking shoes.

Her hair, an orangish-yellow color not seen in nature, was in a huge beehive. Her badge said her name was Flo. I had to resist the urge to ask her to say, "Kiss my grits." She was carrying a to-go cup.

"Here's your coffee darlin'" she said in that Kentucky drawl I'd learned to love while living in Louisville. "Sorry, but we don't sell Coke in bottles in here. There's a machine on every floor alongside the ice machine and the snack machine."

While I was paying for the coffee, my phone buzzed. It was a text from Stultz. I'd texted him the night before so he would have our number. It was risky if Bell killed him and/or took his phone because it would be relatively simple to trace where the text had come from, but it was a risk we had to take if we wanted to know where we stood.

When I opened the text, the hair stood up on the back of my neck. It contained just three characters:

"911."

I forwarded the text to Dee, and went to get her Diet Coke out of a machine just down the hall. Dee had clearly gotten the message, because she was packed and sitting on the edge of the bed when I burst through the door.

"Here," I said, handing her the drink and picking up our luggage. "We gotta go—NOW."

"Do you know what happened?"

"No idea," I answered as I knocked on the door adjoining our room to the Tuttles'. "About all we can surmise is that he's alive, or at least that he was a few minutes ago."

Lilith answered the door with a smile, but immediately saw the grave look on my face and her eyes widened.

"Is he coming?" she asked.

"I don't know. Something went wrong. We have to go fast."

Two minutes later, we were at our cars. Two minutes after that, we were on the road. Truthfully, I wasn't sure of our ultimate destination. I was considering New Orleans or thereabouts. I had a former student there who had become a high-powered lawyer and she would be more than willing to help hide us. But I did know that one stop was going to be Mt. Juliet, Tennessee, home of an old and reliable friend. So we took the Bluegrass Parkway south.

"Phones," I said to Dee.

I needed say no more. She pulled the walkie-talkie from the cup holder and keyed the microphone.

"You guys have your walkie on?"

"Yes," said Lilith.

"I need you to do something for me, okay?" said Dee.

"Sure, what?" asked Lilith.

"Get out your phone and remove the SIM card for me. It's under the battery cover on the back of the phone." said Dee with calm authority in her voice.

"Got it," said Lilith.

"Okay, break it in half." said Dee. "Find something heavy and smash it if you can't break it with your hands."

Dead silence.

"Come again?" asked Lilith, clearly perplexed.

"Trust me sweetie, just do it," said Dee.

"Okay, done," Lilith said after about a minute.

"Good," said Dee. "Now roll down your window and chuck the phone, card and all, out. Better yet, throw it hard down onto the highway. The more pieces the better."

I watched through the rearview mirror as Lilith did exactly what Dee had told her. The phone shattered, the pieces skittering toward the guardrail on the edge of the median. Dee then did the

exact same thing with our phone. We were, I hoped, off the grid.

Chapter 28

Being off the grid is surprisingly unhelpful when people know where you are anyway. This road having long stretches of flat, straight road, I saw them coming for several miles. Initially, they were just an indistinct dot in my rearview mirror, but they quickly morphed from one dot to two black SUV's. One in each lane, they slowed a bit as they caught up with us, which was not a good sign. I spurred Ellie a bit to see what would happen. Tuttle, apparently the type to follow the lead car of a convoy closely, sped up to match me, as did both of the vehicles behind him. It was like we were all flying in a backwards L formation. Definitely not a good sign.

"Wake up Dee," I said.

She came out of her slumber slowly and sleepily looked at me.

"Whut?"

"Get on the walkie and tell Johnny to pass us, please."

Suddenly fully awake, she turned around and immediately saw them. Turning back around, she reached for the walkie talkie.

Trying to sound casual, in case the Tuttles hadn't already seen the dark wraiths behind them, she keyed the mic and said:

"Hey guys, you still awake back there?"

"Who can sleep with these idiots tailgating us like this?" answered Johnny.

So they had seen them but were apparently unaware of their significance. Ignorance truly is sometimes bliss, I suppose.

"Well, why don't you guys just pass us and we'll let them tailgate us for a bit."

"Have I mentioned to you lately that you're brilliant?"

"You hadn't told me today." She smiled coolly. "Remind me to reward you when this is over."

I slowed down so Tuttle could pass me without having to floor it. As he cleared my left front bumper and was getting set to merge back in front of me, the SUV in the hammer lane surged forward. I could see the darkly tinted right rear window slide down, allowing the barrel of a rifle to slide out.

"Gun!" I shouted holding out my right hand.

Instantly, my pistol smacked firmly into my open palm. Like a skilled surgical nurse who anticipates the surgeon's next instrument, she had been waiting for me to say it. I was interested to see if she anticipated the next request.

"Wheel," I said.

Her hand was on the steering wheel in a second. Maybe the wrong Shalan had gone into the thug business. Her steering left me free to roll down my window and aim, which I did, at the right front tire of the SUV beside me. Before I could fire my first round, two short bursts of muzzle flash came from the SUV in rapid succession. The back glass of Tuttle's car exploded with the first round. Happily, I'm left-handed and, in all humility, a pretty darn good shot. It took me only two tries to take out the tire, sending the SUV careening out of control onto the shoulder. It skidded sideways, rear end out, and then started flipping. It was about halfway through its second rotation when it folded with a glass-shattering, steel wrenching crash into a concrete bridge abutment. It bucked as it hit the immovable concrete barrier and came to a complete stop on its roof.

I took the wheel back and Dee took over sharpshooter duties. Rolling down her window and taking off her seatbelt, she turned in her seat to take better aim at the second pursuit vehicle, the driver of which was not going to make the same stupid mistake his or her colleague had. I kept a close eye on him through the rearview mirror. He had dark close- cropped hair and aviator sunglasses, which he took off at some point without my noticing. At first I thought he was making evasive maneuvers behind us to avoid the potshots Dee was firing out her window. She had to use her left hand, so she wasn't quite as accurate as normal, but it was mostly luck in this case anyway.

She was having pretty good luck, though, as three of her first four shots hit the windshield. The problem, however, was that the SUV, a Cadillac Escalade, had bullet-proof glass, so her bullets were being wasted. So why was he dodging the bullets? Then it dawned on me that he was not trying to evade Dee's bullets, but was trying to maneuver me into a spot on the road where he could dart past me to get to Tuttle's car. By getting me to go right to keep Dee lined up for good shots, it was his hope that I would leave the left lane, the lane away from Dee's barrage, open for a quick pass before I could recover and attempt another tire shot. When that became clear, I simply straddled the middle line, wobbling just enough to make it nearly impossible to get past me safely on either side, especially at these outrageous speeds.

"Try for the grill," I said just before the Escalade rammed us. It was all I could do to keep Ellie moving straight, as the driver was either smart or skilled enough to hit me off-center. I slammed down the clutch, yanked the gearshift back out of overdrive into 4th gear, and got into the gas enough to break contact just before it could spin me around. I nearly lost control again, though, as the impact pitched Dee off of her knees and into my side. In her effort to stay upright, she tensed every muscle in her body, including those in her trigger finger. Unhappily, her shot was slightly off, as the bullet tore through Ellie's convertible top. That made two ouchies. My heart broke for her a little. For Ellie, not for Dee. Dee didn't have a bullet hole in her top.

Dee righted herself and began peppering the Escalade's grill, only stopping long enough to change clips. It didn't take long to infer that the grill was just as impregnable as the glass, but she kept firing anyway, just to feel like she was doing something, I guess. For all we knew, the thing would withstand a small bomb blast. It hardly mattered. I was fresh out of bombs. All I had was a car that was, at this point, just barely faster than the SUV chasing us and a wife who, for all her accuracy, may as well have been shooting an air rifle. Just as I was thinking we had a stalemate on our hands, the small back glass panel of the car exploded. The SUV decided to go on the offensive. A muscular looking man with a shaven head was leaning out the front passenger window firing at us. Now it was getting interesting. I remember thanking God that these guys were old school and didn't carry Uzis or shoulder-fired rocket launchers. Dee immediately targeted the shooter. Both vehicles were swerving wildly, so neither one's shots were very accurate. Unfortunately, their shooter had an entire car at which to aim, while Dee was limited to trying to take out the guy hanging out the window. Suddenly, two bullets hit the windshield in quick succession, blowing a pair of gaping holes just inches right of where they would need to be to do the same thing to my head. I instantly ducked down and swerved hard right, then left.

The SUV found another gear somehow and started gaining on me again. Before I could evade him, he hammered at my bumper again, sending Dee sprawling against the dashboard and bouncing her head off the windshield. Being the trooper that she was, she bounced right back to the seat and continued her fusillade as I tried to escape the black behemoth, which had apparently gotten hooked to my rear bumper somehow. Jerking the steering wheel wasn't helping, so I tried slamming on the brakes then gunning the gas. That worked, as I popped free and managed to put about ten feet of space between us. Before long, though, he was gaining on me. Another hit and I feared he had us, so I decided to try something I'd seen on an old TV movie. It would only work if I had a working taillight, but I had nothing to lose. I turned on my headlights in the hopes that he would see the taillight come on and think I was slamming on my brakes and back off. I have no idea how, but it worked. The nose of the SUV dove as the driver slammed on the brakes. I guess it was simply a reflex. His braking gave me the chance to put a bit more distance between us and continue my left-right-left evasive maneuvers.

As I jerked the wheel left, two impossibly bad things happened almost simultaneously. First, the engine started sputtering and coughing periodically like it was starting to be starved of gas. Second, Dee screamed and dropped her gun out the window. Apparently, two of the SUV shooter's wild volleys had managed to hit their marks, one blowing a hole in the gas tank and the other a hole, though thankfully a small one, on the edge of my wife's pinkie finger. Dee cradled her injured hand like a wounded animal and assumed the fetal position beside me. We were soon to be dead in the water with no way to stop them from getting past us to their actual quarry.

Another bridge was coming up in the distance, so, as the SUV swerved right, instead of trying to mirror him, I feinted that way but then cut back to the left and let off the gas, bringing the SUV abreast of me. I didn't want to do this with Dee on the impact side, but I didn't have time to switch sides with the SUV and I'm pretty sure they would have said no if I asked if they would trade with me. Time was running out fast because we were running on fumes and the bridge was no more than a few hundred feet away. I knew there was no way I could win this battle on size alone since the Escalade was, at minimum, twice the weight of Ellie, so I was hoping against hope that I could win it with guile and intimidation. I gunned the gas slightly. Thankfully, Ellie found enough gas to respond—faithful to the end. Hoping my timing was perfect, I cut hard right, catching the front left fender of the SUV with Ellie's right rear quarter panel. It sounded like a detonation as the two vehicles met. I would have to mourn the loss of my beloved car later. At the moment I was trying to prevent having to mourn the loss of my even more beloved wife, not to mention my friends in the car ahead of us.

Somehow, the maneuver worked, as the driver veered hard right trying to get away from my car. His eyes grew wide and his arms locked straight in front of him as he realized too late that he was now forced to select between a concrete barrier and a plunge over a steep embankment. I cranked the wheel left and drove the gas pedal nearly through the floor in the hopes that we had enough fuel left to separate us from the now doomed SUV. At first I didn't think we were going to make it, but at the last instant, there was a deafening crack as we surged into a power slide. I didn't have anything left in me to try to control it, so I simply let her slide until she hammered into the concrete wall of the bridge with her already crumpled right rear fender, facing back the way we had just come. The car jolted to a stop just in time for me to see that the other driver, by failing to choose one path or another, ended up getting the worst of both. The front left end of the SUV clipped the end of the bridge, causing the vehicle to violently helicopter left and disappear over the edge and out of sight. This was followed by a long rumbling explosion as the Escalade crashed and tumbled down the nearly vertical bank. After maybe five seconds, silence replaced the roar. I half expected it to blow up like in the movies, but all was quiet.

I don't know how long it took, but I eventually became aware that I still had the steering wheel in a death grip. Prying my fingers loose, I looked with dread to my right, knowing the woman I love more than life itself was dead beside me. I reached over to put my hand on her crumpled body, which was somehow crammed into the miniscule space on the floor between the dashboard and the seat. All I could see was her hunched back and the top of her head. All I could do was pray for God to let her miraculously be alive.

"Dee?" I croaked out, my throat rapidly closing off. It was like I was looking at her through a long dark tunnel that was narrowing by the instant. I feared knowing, but I had to know. Inexplicably, she twitched in response to my hand lightly touching her back. My heart, nearly immobilized by fear, now restarted with a vengeance.

"I'll give you this, Shalan," came her muffled reply as she raised her head slowly, "you sure know how to show a girl a good time."

Chapter 29

After verifying that Dee was, indeed going to live, I got out and ran the few hundred feet to the Tuttles' car. They had pulled off onto the berm and then backed up toward us when it became evident the chase was over.

"Any injuries up here?" I leaned into the passenger window.

"None serious, apparently," said Johnny. "My heart is still racing, though."

Lilith stared straight ahead, eyes wide. "I don't understand why they're doing this. I can't believe Merton would do this. I was almost killed."

"We all were honey," said Johnny, glowering at his wife.

"That's what I meant. I'm just so shocked. How could he do this?"

"Are you both okay?" asked Johnny.

"I'm fine," I answered. "Dee got a little nick, just superficial. And she's pretty banged up from flying around in the car when we hit the bridge, but she'll be okay."

It was a fact that she was in good enough shape to physically recover relatively quickly. What was not yet established was that she was psychologically and emotionally resilient enough to deal well with this event. Up until this time, she had only been involved in the humdrum, day-to-day elements of our job. She'd never even had to pull a gun. Since the previous summer, we had talked at great length about what she should expect and we had done a lot of training with armed and hand-to-hand conflict, but you can't fully prepare for something like this. You can only experience it and then see how you react after. Some people are naturally good at it. Others start out traumatized but get used to it. Others never recover. I hoped I had reason to believe that Dee was a natural, but time would tell. I forced myself to put these thoughts aside and focus on the task at hand, because the present had enough worries of its own.

I asked Johnny to pop his trunk and ran back to Ellie's shattered remains. The trunk was pretty well smashed in, but luckily the latch had sprung on impact with the bridge barrier, so I quickly raked up our luggage, ran it back to their car, crammed it into the trunk, and then told them to hightail it out of there and to stop at the first restaurant or gas station they found.

"What do we do then?" asked Tuttle.

"Wait," I replied. "We'll find you."

They pulled out and were a few hundred yards down the road as the first police cruiser arrived, followed closely by a couple others, an ambulance, and various rescue vehicles. I arrived at the car as the Kentucky state trooper pulled up and exited his car.

"You okay sir?" asked the trooper.

"Yes, I'm fine," I said, "but my wife is pretty banged up. She might need some attention."

"Those folks you were talking with in that other car," said the trooper, "were they with you?"

"No, they just stopped to see if we needed any help, but when they saw you were here, they went on their way."

The trooper, a rail thin ruddy skinned man who wore his Smokey Bear hat tipped low over his forehead, nearly touching the bridge of his flat, wide nose, looked at me doubtfully. Maybe he'd seen that the Tuttles' car had no back window or maybe he'd seen me putting luggage in the trunk. More likely is that he, like me, had seen enough of the world to be suspicious as a matter of course. Dee was attempting to climb over the center console of the car when the trooper opened the door and held out his hand.

"Let me help you, ma'am." He took a completely different tone than the one with which he addressed me.

"Why thank you officer," Dee said, genuinely happy to see him. As she awkwardly extricated herself from Ellie, the trooper apparently spotted my weapon sticking out from under my seat.

"Gun!" he shouted and pulled his weapon. "Freeze, both of you! Sir, get your hands behind your head! Ma'am, you turn around slowly and place both hands on the trunk of the car. Sir, on your knees, please! Now please lie down, face down on the pavement."

I knew that trying to argue with him would only make it worse, so to the ground I went. Within a few seconds, two other troopers had arrived and were alongside the first one, guns drawn.

"Sir, Ma'am," said another trooper, whose shoulder patch indicated he was the ranking officer, "does either of you have a weapon on your person?"

"No sir." I was silently impressed by the fact that he used such good grammar. "My PI license and carry permit are in my wallet. Center console."

The troopers talked quietly among themselves and the one who had arrived first stepped to the car, reached in, fetched my wallet, and found the documents I promised. As all this happened, two ambulances pulled up and disgorged EMT's, one of whom approached the troopers while the other three headed down the bank to the wreckage of the SUV.

"Harry Shalan," read the ranking trooper aloud. "Mr. Shalan, Kentucky state law requires that any handgun you carry in a car must be in your glove box. Why did we find yours under your seat?"

"It started out in my glove box, but when the folks in those two Escalades started trying to kill us, it seemed prudent to try to stop them."

"By yourself?" he asked.

"No, I helped," said Dee. "I'm afraid I lost my weapon in the fracas, though. They shot it out of my hand, if you can believe that."

"And you are, ma'am?" He was taller than the first trooper, and at least fifteen years his senior. He wore his hat higher on his head so that his large roundish grey eyes could be seen clearly. His face, like his eyes, was quite round, though not fat. Crow's feet and laugh lines portrayed a life lived outdoors.

"I'm Dee Shalan, Harry's wife. He's my husband." She was either trying to act like a harmless woman or had a head wound I hadn't noticed.

"Trooper…" said the ranking trooper, looking at the third trooper, a fierce though attractive woman probably in her late twenties. Her hair, blonde with red highlights, was probably in a pageboy cut, though it was hard to say with her cover on.

"Katelyn Todd, sir."

"Todd, frisk Mrs. Shalan, please. Just for due diligence." As she began that, he turned to me. "Sir, I need you to please get up very slowly and lace your hands behind your head. McGee, if you'll search him as well, please."

Searches complete, the ranking trooper, who turned out to be Lieutenant Mike Franks, asked the EMT to check on Dee and then turned to me. As we talked, the EMT, a smallish Latina woman with long, straight dark hair pulled straight back into a ponytail, examined Dee and then cleaned and bandaged her hand where the bullet had grazed her. By the end, they were like old friends, laughing and sharing inside jokes.

"So Mr. Shalan," he said looking me straight in the eye, "what exactly happened here?"

"Well," I said, "we were driving along minding our own business when these two black SUV's tried to run us off the road." Technically true.

"Any idea who these people are or why they were trying to kill you?"

"I've made enemies in my business, so it could be any of several people." Again, technically true. I knew who they were, but that didn't make what I said a lie.

"Reports are that there seemed to be another vehicle involved. Trooper McGee says you were talking to people in a vehicle and that they fled when you saw his cruiser."

"I'm sorry Lieutenant, but I can't help you with that. Those folks stopped when it was all over to make sure we were okay." Yeah, that was just a lie.

The EMT's made it back from checking on the occupants of the SUV. Grimy and out of breath, the first to arrive was a bear of a man, both in size and hairiness. He had wavy, long sandy hair spilling out from under a ball cap, crooked to the side like young guys wear theirs. I wasn't sure if that was by design or simply because he was too tired to fix it. The look was completed by a full-on Grizzly Adams beard. He was at least 6 feet 4 inches tall with broad shoulders and a thick chest. He wiped his brow with a white hankie he'd retrieved from his back left pocket as he reached us. "Everybody's extremely dead down there." I guess that's opposed to mostly dead. He had a surprisingly high-pitched voice. "It's pretty ugly. One fella was ejected through the windshield and the vehicle apparently rolled over him. Guts and grey matter everywhere. Another guy's head was smashed like a pumpkin." Colorful.

"What about the other vehicle?" asked Franks, apparently not taking notice of the graphic description. "Any survivors in that one?"

"One," answered the EMT, "critical. Major blood loss and severe head trauma. Life flight's coming to take him to UK Medical Center."

As if on cue, the helicopter approached, circled once, and then descended to the highway. We were too far away to see anything, but we all stopped to watch anyway until the chopper again lifted off a few minutes later and flew back north toward Lexington and the trauma center.

"So," said Franks, finally breaking the silence, "Mr. and Mrs. Shalan, what brings you two to our fair commonwealth? I can't help noticing that you're mighty far away from home without luggage." Moving our stuff to their car was a rookie move. Raised questions to which I wouldn't have a plausible answer. Maybe I had a head injury I didn't see.

"That's us." Dee was sitting in the driver's seat of what was left of Ellie. "We're just the spontaneous types. Harry had no paying clients, so we decided to just get in Ellie and take her wherever she went." Have I mentioned I love my wife?

"Ellie?" asked Franks. "Short for Eleanor?

"*Gone in Sixty Seconds*," I said, with a wistful smile. "One of my favorites, just because of the car."

Franks smiled sadly in commiseration, but then continued the interrogation. "Not even a shaving kit or toiletry bag? My ex-wife wouldn't leave home for an hour without her makeup kit, though I would estimate she needed the cosmetics a fair bit more than you do, if I may say so ma'am."

"You're so sweet." Dee gave the Lieutenant her most radiant smile. Even after all this, she was captivating. Franks was made of sterner stuff than I because it wasn't even aimed at me and my stomach became pudding as all my blood rushed to the center of my body, but somehow he managed to resist disrobing and throwing himself on her.

"No ma'am, just observant. No offense, Mr. Shalan."

"None taken. She's bewitched better men than you and I. But anyway, it was spur of the moment and we were just going to buy some things when we got wherever we ended up."

This story started thin and we both knew it. But after a pause, Franks nodded, almost imperceptibly, and called Trooper Todd over. "What's the status on the wrecker for Ms. Ellie here?"

"It's five minutes out, sir," she answered quickly. Good cop. Knew he would ask and had an answer ready.

"Take these fine folks up to the next exit. I imagine they could use a hot shower and a good meal. There's a nice little diner and a bed-and-breakfast just a mile or two off of the highway. Sorry, there's little by way of shopping there, but there's a little shop connected to the diner. You might at least get a hairbrush and toothpaste and such."

Dee looked at me concerned, but I barely shook my head, trying not to be too obvious. She looked away from me and turned her attention to her new friend, Katelyn Todd. Dee got from her father an innate sense that all strangers were simply friends she hadn't met yet. You had to actually try not to like her and even the most curmudgeonly types generally failed, no matter how hard they tried, not to be drawn to her. It had its drawbacks, though—I hated shopping with her since she started a conversation in nearly every aisle.

"So, Trooper Todd" she asked, "you wouldn't happen to have a brush on you, would you? My hair is a disaster area."

"Please, call me Kate," replied the trooper, suddenly morphing from stern and professional to light and congenial, "and yes, I've got one in my cruiser. Come right on over here with me."

I followed along despite not being invited because, well, I needed a ride too. When we got to Trooper Todd's car, Dee got in the front passenger seat, which left me to climb in the back, behind the cage. I wish I could say this was the first time I'd seen life from this side of a police car, but at least this time I got in voluntarily.

The trooper and Dee chatted like they'd gone to college together. Dee asked how she liked being a state trooper, to which Katelyn replied that it was fine, but what she really wanted was to work in the FBI or even Secret Service. Her real dream was be assigned to guard the president. "Can you imagine flying on Air Force One?"

"No, sweetie, I can't imagine flying again after my last flight."

"What happened?"

I was afraid Dee would give away too much information, but I shouldn't have worried. She's so much smarter than I give her credit for.

"My arrival was delayed for so long that I felt like I was being held prisoner. Some of the folks I dealt with were so rude, but thankfully, a supervisor showed up and helped get the whole situation straightened out."

I chuckled to myself at the fact that every single thing Dee said was accurate but that none of it was really true. Again, I wondered where she had developed all these skills. Maybe she was a

deep cover government agent. As we slowed to pull onto the exit, I

spied the Tuttles' car in the parking lot of a McDonald's. I leaned

forward and blurted out the first thing that came into my head.

"Umm, Katelyn, could we stop at that MickeyD's. I really gotta'

go."

"It's only a couple more miles to the diner." She sounded

like an impatient parent. Appropriate. Dee always accuses me of

being an overgrown eight-year-old.

"I may not make it that far!"

"Okay," she said, and whipped her cruiser into the restaurant

parking lot.

I waited anxiously as she got out of the car and let me out.

Stupid cop cars and their no handles on the inside. Upon release, I

leapt out of the car and bolted for the nearest door inside. I was

doing my best to sell this, but I didn't need to try all that hard. I

actually did have to go. Once inside, though, I spied Johnny and

Lilith sitting at a booth sipping at drinks. Lilith was staring into her

empty soft drink cup and didn't take note of me, though she did steal

an occasional furtive glance at Johnny. She looked exhausted and something else, though I couldn't place what. Johnny saw me and started to get up, but I quickly shook my head and held out my hand subtly in front of me to signal him to stop. He caught my intent and made out like he was going for extra napkins. As he walked toward the counter, I nodded ever so slightly toward the restroom. He gave one small nod in ascent. I was thankful that the trooper who drove us was a woman so we could go in there without worrying about being joined by the authorities.

I then made a beeline for the bathroom. Before I could completely finish my business, the door opened. It was Johnny. He waited until I was all zipped up and washing my hands before talking to me. It's a rule. All guys know it.

"So what happened? Do the police want to talk to us? I assume not since we're doing this subterfuge thing. I saw that a state trooper brought you here."

"I managed to keep you out of the story. How's Lilith? She seemed pretty rattled back there."

"She's calmer now. The whole time we were driving here and then after we got here, she just kept saying, 'I can't believe it, I can't believe it.' But she went to the bathroom and was much calmer when she got back."

"Good. Now here's what I want you to do. Make note of which way we go when we leave, which should be right. Wait about twenty minutes and go the same way. The trooper's taking us to a diner and bed-and-breakfast. Hopefully they're on the main road. If you go more than two miles, turn back and look for signs. If the cruiser is still there when you find it, just drive by and wait a bit. Once we can get together alone, we'll figure out where to go from here."

Tuttle nodded his head and went back out. I waited about thirty seconds and went out myself, only to be greeted by Trooper Todd laughing raucously coming out of the women's restroom, followed closely by Dee, also boisterously laughing. Always in groups. That's a rule too, I guess.

Chapter 30

Katelyn Todd took us to the diner, going in and making sure the woman behind the counter knew that we were crime victims and should be treated like special guests. She then asked the lady, who looked familiar to me, though I couldn't figure out why, for double cheeseburger with everything, a large fries, and chocolate shake extra thick to go. Apparently, she was a regular, because they had her order almost before she asked for it.

"Thanks, Bettie," The name told me why I recognized the counter lady. "Put this on my tab, would you?"

"Sure thing doll." She had that fluid smoker's throat.

"Whatever else you get," Katelyn Todd said to us, "make sure to get a chocolate shake, extra thick. Best thing ever."

Before she left, she shook my hand, and then gave Dee a quick hug and handed her a card with her name, the phone number to her station, and her extension. On the back, she had hand-written her cell number and email address.

"You need anything or think of anything helpful, please call. And don't forget you promised me that book on training Boxer puppies. My Tony is a terror."

"I won't forget—thank you so much Katelyn."

We walked her back out to her cruiser and waved fondly as she pulled out, heading down the road away from the entrance to the Bluegrass Parkway. Must have been sent on another call. We went back in and took a four-top booth away from the window. Dee ordered sweet tea and I ordered mine unsweetened. I have come to believe that good tea, hot or iced, requires no sweetener at all. Emphasis on the word good, which, I am happy to report, this was. After she brought us our drinks, we told our waitress that we would wait to order lunch until our friends arrived, so she told us just to wave her down when we were ready or wanted a refill.

After she left, I looked around. The diner had that retro 50s look, though based on the age of the place, it may actually have been built in the 50s, never been renovated, and had come back around to being cool again. Like many older diners, it was modeled after the originals, which had been old railroad cars that had been re-purposed; therefore, it was long and narrow, with just enough room

for a row of booths, a narrow aisle and the stools in front of the bar.
The stainless steel stools were anchored to the floor and were
covered on top with slightly worn and cracked brown Naugahyde
cushions. Behind the bar were the grill top, deep fryer, various
refrigerators, shake makers, fountain drink dispensers, giant tea urns,
and coffee pots that one associates with a diner. All around the room,
there were framed pictures of curvy, long-legged pin-up girls in
various stages of undress. Above the counter on the wall were menu
items on those felt boards with grooves for letters on either side of a
Dr. Pepper clock with only the 10, 2, and 4 on the dial. It was the
exact same clock that was over the counter in the corner grocery
store that I frequented as a kid.

Suddenly, I was back at Ludwig's Market. It was a dark old
place that was always cool because of the ceiling fans that lined the
long room; they sold a little bit of everything there, from groceries to
hardware to household cleaners, even some clothing. But I never got
anything but candy or pop. I could still taste the Clark Bars and see
the designs on the bottles. Frostie had a picture of what I thought
was Ol' Man Winter smiling gleefully atop a cold frosty mug of root
beer. Mountain Dew, had an image of a hillbilly having a hole shot

in the brim of his tattered hat by the exploding cork from a jug of moonshine with the motto, "It'll tickle yore innards!"

Slowly drifting back to present day, I looked at the menu, which didn't appear to have changed for a while, though I'm sure the prices had. It was burgers, fries, malteds, shakes, soft drinks, ice cream, and fresh homemade pies and cakes, which were contained in a rotating display on the bar just beneath the clock. I had my eye on what appeared to be peanut butter pie. It was going to be a struggle to concentrate on anything else until I wrapped my lips around that.

Beyond the menu on the left was a dry erase board containing specials written quite neatly in green marker. Today's were grilled cheese with homemade tomato soup and Derby Pie. Opposite that on the far right of the menu was a bulletin board containing flyers for various local events and an ad for a car for sale. The car looked to be a dark colored (no way to know exactly from the black-and-white printout) 80s model Crown Victoria. Beneath the picture, written in hand, was "$1500 OBO." The flyer had those little tabs cut on the bottom with phone numbers. The bar and all tables had white Formica countertops that might well have been original equipment, though they were meticulously maintained. The facing of the bar was made up of white ceramic tile set in a diamond pattern punctuated by a red tile every few feet. There was a stainless steel foot rail that ran the length of the bar. I noted with satisfaction that even that was kept quite clean.

There was a miniature jukebox at every table stocked with 45's from the 50s and early 60s. I turned the wheel on the front to scroll through the selection, stopping at two facing pages containing several tunes by Frank Sinatra, Bobby Darin, and Dean Martin. Fishing in my pocket, I was distraught to find I had no change. Before I could ask, Dee reached into her purse and slid a quarter across the table. Gleefully, I dropped the coin and made my three selections: "Three Coins in the Fountain" by Sinatra, "Beyond the Sea" by Darin, and "That's Amoré" by Dean Martin.

I got the impression the lady behind the counter came with the place when it opened. She was perhaps 75, but an energetic 75 to be sure. Her hair was between brown and black, though that was clearly not her real color (at least not anymore), with straight bangs in front and long in the back. Her cheeks had grown slightly jowly with age, but she still had an hourglass figure and it was clear she was a looker when she was younger. In a different, more mature

way, she still was.

"How y'all doin'?" she asked us convivially from behind the

counter as she cleaned away the dishes from a recently departed

diner.

"Not bad, all things considered," I answered. "How are you

Ms. Page?"

"Not many people as young as you have even heard the name

Bettie Page," she said with a huge grin, "let alone know what she

looks like. I've idolized her since I was a little girl. She wasn't

famous yet when I was born, but I always believed it was no

coincidence my folks named me Bettie. Aren't you a sweetie!"

"Nah, I just know a pin-up girl when I see her."

"Not anymore, honey, but once, a lifetime ago. Least my

photographer ex-husband thought so. Notice anything about those

photos on the walls?"

Looking closely for the first time at the three close enough

for me to see, I realized they were all of the same woman—a

younger version of the lady behind the counter. She wore a platinum blonde wig in one, but the face and build were unmistakable. I let out a long, lascivious whistle. "I was born too late."

"Umm," said Dee, "hello? Remember me—the wife?"

"Oh, honey, I'm just expressing appreciation for the female form, of which yours is obviously second to none."

"Keep diggin' doll," said Bettie, winking at Dee. "Let me know when you get to China."

I smiled weakly at Dee, who tried to look angry, but I could see the mirth at the edges of her mouth and in her eyes. At any rate, before I could get myself in even more trouble, the Tuttles saved me by walking through the front door. Defying the realms of possibility, Johnny took one look at the woman behind the counter and exclaimed:

"Wow—Bettie Page!"

Everyone in the diner, except Johnny and Lilith, burst into laughter.

Chapter 31

Dinner was quite pleasant, including the peanut butter pie. Dee reached over and forked off a bite and I nearly gouged her. Like Joey Tribbiani, Harry doesn't share food—especially homemade peanut butter pie that is so indescribably delectable that it could make a mother sell her favorite child for just one more piece. But one simply does not stab one's wife over food. I actually debated with myself over licking the plate when it was finished, especially since I lost a bite to Dee, but I gave in to social convention yet again and settled for fantasizing about it. I was so full, though, that I could barely leave my seat when it was time to waddle out. I would definitely need to put in an extra couple miles in the morning. Like a hundred or so.

We sat so long we cleared the place out, so when she got her counter squared away for the upcoming dinner rush, Bettie Page, whose name turned out to be Bettie Ruble, pulled up a chair and chatted with us for about a half hour, flirting shamelessly with me. I even flirted back a little, making sure that Dee noticed. Fair recompense for that bite of pie. For the briefest period, we forgot that we were on the run, that someone else might be lying in wait around the next corner. It didn't even occur to us that the police would probably look askance at the fact that we were together with this couple who we said were anonymous good Samaritans.

We sat so long, ate so much, and were so exhausted by the events of the day that we decided to stop for the night and try to check in to the bed and breakfast, despite the fact that it was not even 3:00PM yet. While Johnny and Lilith brought the car around, Dee and I decided to walk since our destination was just a couple blocks behind the diner. Before we left, I went to the bulletin board at the right end of the bar and grabbed a phone number tab off the bottom of the car sale flyer.

The inn was a grand old two-story house in the Greek revival style. It was all white with four columns supporting the front of the roof, which extended over a second floor veranda, which in turn stood over the front section of a first floor porch that wrapped almost entirely around three sides. High atop the house was a glass-enclosed lookout area I was later told by the innkeeper was called a promenade deck.

The interior was just as grand, with dark, rich hardwood floors stretching from the entry hall all the way down the corridor past a staircase with the same dark hardwood treads and contrasting white risers, to the back of the house, where the check-in area was. The archway leading from the entryway into the main hallway, along with all of the woodwork in the house, all painted white, was complemented by understated floral wallpaper. The paper's buff background was offset by blue hydrangea blossoms.

Although they normally would be completely booked up due to the fact that it was still a holiday weekend, because of a last-minute cancellation, they had but one room available and it only had one queen-sized bed. We were being checked in by the owner, a man who looked like he could easily play Robert E. Lee in a Civil War re-enactment. This effect was heightened by his slow southern drawl and bourbon-laden breath. He informed us that they had one rollaway bed that we could use at no extra charge since we were paying cash. It wasn't ideal but it was much better than the alternative, driving on. Aside from being too tired to travel, it was not advisable to continue driving the Tuttles' car, since it was known to Bell's men.

Checked in and paid up, we all went to the car for luggage and then headed to the room. The rollaway was already there and set up. The room was large, so it was still possible to move around comfortably. Actually, large doesn't quite do it justice. Cavernous, maybe. It appeared someone had taken two or maybe even three rooms that were on the front of the house and made them into one huge space. It wasn't quite big enough to play tennis in, but maybe racquetball.

We dropped our luggage and collapsed onto our beds, but not until we argued over who got the rollaway. The Tuttles finally assented to taking the big bed since it had better support and Johnny had a notoriously bad back. Even back when I was in college, he would clearly be miserable many days in class and would even have to cancel class from time to time because he couldn't get out of bed. He had had surgery, but it brought, he said, only marginal relief. So they lay down on the beautiful white duvet (probably not appropriate to the period of the house, but quite comfortable nonetheless) while we stretched out on the rollaway, which was somewhat cramped but surprisingly comfortable and supportive. Dee always lies practically on top of me anyway, no matter how big the bed is, so this was the better bed for us. Enervation combined with an inordinate amount of carbohydrates for lunch overwhelmed the other three, so they were snoozing within minutes. Sleep eluded me, however, as I couldn't stop thinking that we might be endangering ourselves by not staying on the move. But moving on in a known vehicle was just as dangerous, so I decided to get up and try to do something about that.

There was a phone in the room, but I didn't want to wake everyone, so I slipped my shoes on and headed out and down to the front desk. I found there that General Lee had been replaced by a man many years his junior, though the family resemblance was unmistakable. Same thick hair, though parted higher on his head. No need for a comb over quite yet. The beard was much more pepper than salt, whereas the elder's was salt nearly to the exclusion of its sister spice. I'd never seen a picture, but I imagined that was what Cadet Lee would have looked like at West Point. I assumed he was the general's son, though he could have been a much younger brother.

"Hello sir." It was nearly the identical baritone voice and warm southern drawl. There were several years less bourbon in it. "How may I help you?"

"Hi. Is there a phone I could use? I hope it's a local call."

I pulled the slip of paper from my pocket and showed it to him. His unkempt eyebrows shot up to become bushy horizontal parentheses and he smiled warmly, revealing straight teeth somewhat yellowed by smoking the pipe he held unlit in his right hand. Upon drawing near to him, I was taken back to my childhood when my father took up the pipe as an interim step between cigarettes and quitting altogether. I still recall with shock the day Dad let me take a draw off his pipe and being dumbfounded that something with such a rich, glorious aroma could taste so much like burnt rubber and urine. Like someone took a leak on a tire fire. At any rate, as he handed me back the slip of paper, his smile became conspiratorial and was accompanied by a wink. It seemed he knew this number and was enjoying being part of some sort of intrigue in talking with me about it.

"Yes sir that is a local number. In fact, I know these folks as well as the car they are selling. It's somewhat advanced in age but quite well maintained, out of necessity. Should serve you well. I'm of the impression that you may be in need of some level of discretion, so you've chosen wisely. Tell them that C. E. Winchester said so and they'll give you a fine deal. There's a phone in the parlor. Through that door behind you to the right."

A little nonplussed by how perceptive Cadet Lee was, I nodded thanks and stepped into the parlor. It was as lovely as the rest of the house, though the wallpaper, metallic copper with a large red rose blossom motif, was a little loud for my taste. It struck me as something one might find in an old brothel. The furniture, a large sofa, loveseat, and three uncomfortable looking armchairs matched some element of the wallpaper. The couch was a less harsh version of the gold, while the loveseat was dusty rose and the armchairs were the same green as the stems and leaves. At the far end of the room was huge fireplace with a stone hearth and a cherry mantel. There was a small fire burning, but when I looked more closely, I was appalled to find it had been converted to a gas log. The most striking feature of the room was without question the mammoth bay window that looked out over what would, in summer, be a lovely circular rose garden. Even with the roses cut back and hooded in chicken wire cylinders filled with leaves for insulation, the garden itself was quite handsome. Maybe thirty feet across, it was bordered with old bricks half buried at a slight angle. At ninety degree intervals, the circle was broken by pathways into the center, where a 6-foot oak swing hung from a white wooden frame. Opposite the swing were two white wicker chairs with forest green cushions. In between was a low oblong coffee table of the same white wicker. At the end of the path opposite me was a white arbor, beyond which a path meandered back and forth in a lazy S before disappearing over a slight hillock, only to reappear a short distance later at the edge of the woods a few hundred yards beyond the house. The floor of the walkways was pea gravel, while the areas around the roses were filled with cedar mulch.

I wondered if I was calling the local bootlegger as I dialed the number on a faux antique desk phone with a tall metal switch hook into which the handset nested. It had an oak base and was trimmed out in bronze. The handset had the same oak and bronze on the handle and the ear and mouth pieces. Except for the fact that the hand crank on the side was purely decorative (I spun it around a few times just because I couldn't not do it) and that the dial was actually a round touch pad, it looked just like an antique phone. Partway through the third ring, I was quite thrilled by the accent on the other end of the line.

"Allo, whatcherwant?" said the booming, gravelly voice in a thick Cockney accent.

"Hello. I'm calling about the car you have advertised. I saw your flyer at the local diner and C. E. Winchester here at the Beauregard Inn told me you could give me a good deal."

"Oh he did, did he?" The voice boomed with mirth. "Well, we can fix you right up. Be over in a jif. Mind, you're not with the coppers are you?"

"Umm, coppers, no. In fact, I'd rather the coppers not get wind of this if you don't mind."

"Fine by me!" He let loose a booming laugh.

I hoped his level of discretion didn't match his level of subtlety, though I already liked this guy. I hoped he looked like he sounded. A few minutes later, when he pulled up and climbed out of the car, I was transfixed to be greeted by the living embodiment of a mythical giant. He was at least 6 feet 8 inches tall and just as wide, had long, wildly bushy black hair and a beard to match, and was wearing an ankle length black wool trench coat over a grey sweatshirt, that could have been used as a tent if one sewed up the neck hole and sleeves, well-worn thick canvas pants at least six inches too short, and leather boots that would have made the Old Woman in the Shoe envious. He reached out a hand that would make a bear paw seem diminutive, and shook mine. When I say shook, I actually mean mangled. It was worth every pulverized knuckle, though.

"Allo, Rubeus Coltrane is the name," he said with a great toothy grin that shone out from the thick shrubbery of his facial hair.

"Hi, I'm Harry."

"Wouldn't be Harry Potter, would it?" He nearly shattered the windows on the front of the inn with his belly laugh.

"No, not Potter. But I take it you know you look just like Hagrid?"

"That's actually my real name. Oops, I shouldn't a said that."

We both laughed hard. The entire time we talked, I couldn't stop smiling and I had to fight an overwhelming urge to hug this human mountain. I felt like I was in the presence of a beloved friend I'd met for the first time in person, though I'd known him for years. I wouldn't have been surprised to see Hermione and Ron sitting in the backseat of his car with Harry riding shotgun.

"So you need a car, eh?" he asked.

"Yes, I'm afraid mine is pretty beat up," I answered.

"That wouldn't a been your car that I towed to me shop yesterday, would it? Mustang convertible, looked like it had been dropped off a building?"

"That would be her," I said despondently.

"Shame that is. She looked like she was a beauty."

"Oh, she was that. Saw me through some rough times. Died before her time."

"Well, we'll see what we can do 'bout that, won't we?"

I was certain there was nothing we could do about that, but it was a pretty thought anyway. In the meantime, we had a deal to transact. I walked over and examined the Grand Marquis. It was solid black with crimson crushed velvet upholstery inside. It felt a little like a cross between a tank and the Batmobile. Definitely enough room for the four of us to ride comfortably, along with half the population of Parkersburg.

"How many miles on her?" I noted with satisfaction that the black sidewall tires had plenty of tread.

"Oh, she's well beyond a hundred thousand, she is, but don't let that bother you. She's good for another hundred easy. New shocks, new brakes, new muffler, new tires, new belts, and new hoses. Changed the oil every three thousand miles and she's never leaked a drop of oil in her life."

"Wow, sounds like you really love her. Why are you selling her?"

"Well, me main business keeps me terrible busy these days and I'm not getting any younger, so I decided it's time to retire from me side business. Too many late hours and too many of the wrong type a people, if you know what I mean."

I wanted very badly to ask him what his side business was, but thought better of it. As I circled the car, I was honestly shocked by how showroom new it looked. No chipped paint anywhere, no signs of rust, and every piece of chrome was polished to a mirror-like state.

"I love this car," I said. "In fact, I feel a little guilty about how I feel toward this car so soon, but Ellie would've wanted me to move on. I want to buy her from you, but I have a slight problem. Two, actually. First, I need to drive her away today with legitimate tags so I won't draw any undue attention from the coppers, as you call them."

"I thought you said you had a problem. Legal plates on her already, no extra charge. Trust me—if the coppers run a check, they'll come back clean as a whistle. Now, your second problem?"

"I'm here with friends who have a car that we need to get rid of. It's missing some glass, but is in pretty good shape other than that. Would you consider taking it in trade?"

He knitted his giant brow and his hand disappeared into his thicket of beard as he scratched his chin. After ruminating a few seconds, he nodded his head.

"Let's have a look at her first, but I'm not against a trade in principle."

We walked together around to the back parking lot. Normally reserved for staff, we had gotten permission to park there. I had moved the car myself, so I had the keys in my pocket. I handed him the keys and he looked it over for just a few seconds before nodding his acceptance of the deal.

"Won't take much work and I can sell her for four times what the Marquis is worth. You sure I can't sweeten the deal for you at all?"

"Believe me, you've more than done your part."

I kept waiting for Ashton Kutcher to come out from behind the bushes to tell me I was being punked, but finally decided that this deal was not, in fact, too good to be true. So I risked further disfigurement by extending my hand, which he took and shook so hard that I was waiting to see my arm fly off at the shoulder. He let me look around inside the car to gather anything we hadn't already unpacked. After I was satisfied that all of our personal belongings were removed, he somehow shoehorned himself into the driver's seat and fired the engine. Through the window, my new old friend handed me the keys to my new tankmobile with an ornery grin.

"Whenever you get the chance, stop by me garage. Me shop is just a couple blocks away. Can't miss it."

And just like that, Hagrid was gone. It was, up to that time, quite possibly the most magical moment of my life. Now all I had to do was explain to the Tuttles that I had just traded away their car.

Chapter 32

They took it better than I thought. What they didn't take all that well was our departure time the next morning: 5:00am. Dee was even less thrilled. "Is there even such a thing as a five o'clock in the morning? I knew there was a PM one, but I've never seen an AM one and I'm not interested in seeing it now."

"What are you squalling about? You'll be asleep by the time I get the car started."

Eventually they all acceded to my logic that we needed to be out of town before the police came back or, even more urgently, before Bell sent reinforcements, and that we were pushing our luck by staying overnight at all. By then, we were all hungry again, so we headed back over to Bettie's Diner. Bettie apparently never didn't work because she was still there behind the counter, but had little time for more than a hello, this being the supper rush. Despite the place being packed to the rafters, our service was quick and friendly, and the food was all scrumptious. I had a grilled chicken salad and forewent the pie this time. We lingered at our table for a few minutes too long, though, as Lieutenant Mike Franks and Trooper Timothy

McGee walked through the door just as we were rising from our seats.

"Hi Bettie," said Franks. "I see you've met the Shalans, and the, uh…"

"Tuttles," said Johnny after an awkwardly pregnant pause. "I'm Johnny and this is my wife Lilith."

"Thought you told us you didn't know these folks." McGee, without his trooper hat on, now looked about 15. His dirty blonde hair was in a buzz cut.

"Well, we don't," I said, trying to cover my tracks. "Or we didn't. It was a happy coincidence that they walked in here."

I knew as soon as I said it that they'd never buy it. No good detective believes in coincidence, especially one as gargantuan as this one. I guess this might be one of those times when lying to the police would actually make things harder for my client. All rules have exceptions, sadly, and this appeared to be one of them.

"You wouldn't happen to be most recently from Chicago, would you, Mr. and Mrs. Tuttle?" Franks casually sat on a stool directly across from our table and leaned his elbows on the bar behind him. His pose reminded me of a cowboy leaning against a bar in an old western saloon.

"How did you know?" asked Lilith.

"Police. We find stuff out. Ran checks on all those folks you, um dealt with, Mr. Shalan. Pretty impressive, by the way. Eight professional assassins in a couple of armored SUV's against a couple of private eyes from a small town in West Virginia, one who looks more suited for modeling than detective work and who's had her PI license for a grand total of four months, and you managed to kill 7 of the eight and most likely turn the eighth into a vegetable. They were from Chicago, reputed to be in the employ of one Merton Bell, though that isn't, of course, legally provable. We do know that his son had a live-in private tutor named, interestingly enough, Jonathan Tuttle."

McGee, satisfied that they were going to be there a while, sat at the stool to Franks' right and ordered a slice of peanut butter pie with decaf coffee. I was overcome with jealousy. How could he do that to me? Even worse, how could the pie shamelessly throw itself at him right in front of me after all we'd meant to each other just a few hours ago. Before I could pull my gun, Dee seemed to sense my intentions and grabbed my right hand in both of hers.

"Upon further investigation, we discovered that, back in the early nineties, Mr. Tuttle here was Professor Tuttle at a small college in West Virginia, uh, let's see." He pulled a small spiral notebook from his right rear pocket and flipped through some pages. "Glenville State College, alma mater of one Harry D. Shalan, who majored in English, Tuttle's subject. Staggering number of coincidences."

"Impressive," I said.

"Just gumshoe work," replied Franks. "Hardly compares to your exploits on the Parkway. But that brings us to the question of why you lied to us. The police frown on being lied to."

I finally decided we had no choice but to come clean. "Okay, you got us. I was attempting to keep the Tuttles out of this because I'm trying to protect them. Yes, Johnny worked for Merton Bell, but not by choice. Bell had some—well let's just say he had some leverage on him—but while he did pay him well, it was with the understanding that he had no choice. It was stay in his employ or he and his family would regret it. So they ran to us. Until we get Bell to back off, I'm trying to keep them alive."

"Why not go to the police?"

"Johnny knew several cops on Bell's payroll. Be like reporting a fox to a coyote."

"But why not tell me? I'm not an employee of Merton Bell. And, after all, 'Mine honor is my life; both grow in one; Take honor from me, and my life is done.'"

"How did I know that? I'm only telling you this because it appears you have us cornered. It's quite simple to, 'Look like the innocent flower, But be the serpent under 't.'"

"Should've known better than to quote Shakespeare to an old English teacher."

"Former. Old sounds creaky."

"Okay. What's your plan to keep this former employee of Merton Bell and his missus from being formerly living?"

"At the moment we're in firefighter mode. Somebody tries to light us up, we endeavor to put them out. The plan was someone on the inside I was hoping could help, but I fear he's been, if you'll pardon the pun, extinguished."

"So what would you like from me?"

"There is one thing. We'd love to stay here overnight just to get some rest. We've been on the run for a couple days. Lot less fun than it sounds. Spare someone to keep an eye on the Beauregard until we leave?"

"I know just the person for the job."

"Does that mean we can sleep in?" asked Dee.

"It would appear so, Red," said Franks. "You mind if I call you Red?"

"Oh, thank you sweet baby Jesus! You can call me anything you want as long as you don't call me early tomorrow morning!"

Franks smiled at Dee a little longer than I liked, but turned to me just in time so avert a punch in the throat. "Think you can keep everyone breathing for an hour or two until I can make the arrangements?"

"I'll do my best Lieutenant."

"I'd say your best is probably good enough." Franks turned to McGee, who had apparently finished his dessert and was on about his third cup of decaf. I felt small for it, but I caught myself hoping Bettie had sensed my anguish and, in a gesture of solidarity, slipped him regular coffee so that he'd toss and turn all night. Franks nodded toward the door and the two troopers made their exit.

As we were rising to head back to the Beauregard, I glanced over at the bar and to my total disbelief, Trooper McGee had left at least two bites of pie on his plate. I wished I'd shot him when I had the chance because the life of anyone who would voluntarily not finish that unutterable wedge of joy wasn't worth living anyway. I wondered if people would think ill of me if I went over there and polished it off. Wouldn't everyone agree that it's a crime against all that's good in the world to just throw it away? Dee, again knowing me too well, pulled me toward the door.

"Don't even think about it!"

I guess not everyone.

Chapter 33

Much to my wife's delight, Lieutenant Franks had sent us Katelyn Todd. She had apparently gone home and changed into her civilian clothes; I didn't recognize her at all through the peephole and barely recognized her when I opened the door. Gone were all the stern police appearance and demeanor. It was replaced by a genuinely lovely young woman with a white smile that was open and honest. Her hair, which did turn out to be in a pageboy, was shiny, with the red highlights more pronounced. She probably washed it when she got home to get rid of the hat hair. As I ushered her in, I caught the subtle hint of something floral, maybe Romance by Ralph Lauren, though I'd only smelled that once while Christmas shopping with Dee. Whatever the brand, it was understated and extremely feminine. While clearly chosen for comfort and ease of movement, her clothes showed off her trim, fit figure. Under her uniform overcoat, her top was a black cow neck sweater, and her jeans were midrise. Not mom jeans, but not the low cut skinny jeans so many teenagers and people who aren't anticipating the possibility of armed pursuit tend to wear. A perfect combination of function and modesty, they also showed off the fact that she was well built and kept herself in shape. I guessed she was a runner, an inference strengthened by the fact that she wore fuchsia and dusty grey Saucony running shoes. She wore my brand. Pretty and smart.

"Kate!" exclaimed Dee. "I was hoping it would be you!"

"I insisted." Katelyn exchanged hugs with my wife.

"Trooper Katelyn Todd," said Dee, "this is Jonathan Tuttle and his lovely wife Lilith."

The three exchanged handshakes and pleasantries, after which Katelyn turned to me. "So how do you want me to play this? Stake out the place from outside or stay inside so I can get to your room quickly?"

"There are two entrances, one in the back leading into the kitchen, plus all the ground floor windows, so you can't go it alone. Dee and I could take turns covering the back while you watch the front."

She had apparently anticipated my idea, as she handed me an extra walkie talkie. "Being subtle or making it clear you're being guarded?"

"Not spy-level, but let's not announce ourselves. Maybe if we're careful, we can catch a mouse instead of sqhishing its little head."

"I'll hang around a few minutes and then circle the house like I'm checking in on you and then head out. When I leave, I'll pull in around the back of the diner. I can park in behind the dumpster without being too obvious and still have an unobstructed view of the front and east side of the inn."

Plans made, Katelyn focused her attention on visiting with Dee and getting to know Johnny and Lilith. I didn't pay much attention to the discussion, though it seemed light and cordial. I was too restless to sit and chat, so I went to my luggage to retrieve my spare weapon for Dee, after which I cleaned my gun. It needed it anyway, but cleaning a gun always calms my mind.

As I put away my cleaning supplies, Katelyn, undoubtedly waiting to make sure I was ready, rose to say her goodbyes. Hugging Dee, and shaking hands again with Johnny and Lilith, she headed toward the door.

"I'll walk you out and take up my position too," I said, donning my coat and checking to make sure my toboggan cap and gloves were still in the pockets.

Dee rose, crossed the room, and wrapped her arms around me, placing her open palms on the small of my back; she kissed me gently on the lips, and then laid her head against my chest. I engulfed her in my arms, laying my cheek on the top of her head.

"You be careful Mister Man."

"Careful is my middle name."

"And all this time I thought it was Dean." She kissed me and smiled. "When shall I relieve you?"

"I'll come get you when I get sleepy,"

"No you won't." I hated and loved that I was absolutely no mystery to this woman. "I'll set my alarm for two and be out shortly thereafter."

"Fine then." I kissed her on top of the head as I broke our embrace.

"Talk to you soon Kate," said Dee as we opened the door and started toward the steps, Katelyn in front of me.

The night was dark, with ominous, black, roiling clouds hanging low in the sky as if they were waiting to see what might happen and were fighting for a close enough spot to get a good look. The air felt cold and damp, but the temperature hovered at least fifteen degrees above the freezing mark. The National Weather Service was calling for heavy rain toward morning, but it felt and smelled like it might be coming sooner rather than later. Rain was a double-edged sword on a stakeout. It made the stakers less visible, but it also helped conceal the stake-ees.

"I'll let you know when I'm in position," said Katelyn after we'd circled the house. She climbed into her vehicle, a late model Jeep Grand Cherokee that I could only tell in the extremely low light was dark colored.

I waved as she pulled out and watched her drive away, then took the gravel path around the house, through the rose garden, and then turned right, walked through the arbor I'd seen that afternoon, and on into the woods. About fifty yards in, I left the path. Pulling a small Maglite from my hip pocket, I headed west a few hundred yards until I estimated I had come even with the back of the Beauregard Inn and then made my way to the small lawn at the back of the property. The going was pretty easy, as the woods were cleared of most of the underbrush. As I neared the edge of the woods, I paused to make sure no one was around, then killed the flashlight and jogged the hundred feet or so to the Tankmobile, which I had moved to the back employee parking lot after Hagrid left. My walkie crackled to life as I was climbing into the driver's seat.

"Mr. Shalan, this is Trooper Todd, I'm in position." Her voice was flat and tinny over the small speaker.

"How about we go with Harry and Katelyn? You're off duty and I'm your best friend's husband."

"Sounds good." There was laughter in her voice. "But if we're going to be on a first name basis, please call me Kate. There's only one person who ever called me Katelyn and, frankly, he was a very bad man."

There seemed like a compelling story there, but the night was young, so I let it drop for the time being. "Alrighty, Kate it is."

I decided I could probably get used to this car with seats as big and as comfortable as couches. Putting the key in the ignition, I turned on the radio, which was part of an aftermarket Pioneer stereo system with a six-disc CD changer and USB port. I had no CDs and left my mp3 player in the room, so I settled for cruising the radio dial. This was proving fruitless, however, as there didn't seem to be much from which to choose. All the presets simply brought static and the scan button produced a grand total of three stations: one country (ick), one bluegrass (icker), and one heavy metal (ickest). So I tried the tune button, moving slowly from frequency to frequency. After maybe a minute, I found a station, distant but audible, playing Christmas music. Things were looking up. The unmistakable groan of Bing Crosby's familiar dream of a "White Christmas" greeted my happy ears. It was only a few days after Thanksgiving, but, as Auntie Mame once put it, at a time like this, we needed a little Christmas. Eventually, Bing faded away and was replaced, to my near giddy delight, by Michael Bublé's "Jingle Bells" with the Puppini Sisters. I listened contentedly until the song gave way to commercials, then keyed the walkie talkie's mic.

"Hey Kate. You there?"

"Yessir."

"So, what's a beautiful girl like you doing in a place like this?"

There was a pause while I'm sure she was swooning and trying not to drive over here and sexually assault me. Or maybe she was hysterical with laughter.

"Has that line ever worked for anyone?" She chuckled. So it was B.

"I don't know. I never tried it before. Come to think of it, I've never tried a line of any kind on any woman. Didn't date much before Dee and it was clear the night we met that we were a couple, so I never even tried one on her."

"Well thanks for saying I'm beautiful, even if it was just a stupid joke."

"No joke."

"Well thank you." If it's possible to sound like you're blushing, she did.

"I didn't mean to embarrass you. Sorry."

"No it's okay. Just not something I've heard a lot in my life, especially from someone as handsome as yourself."

"Aw, shucks."

"Seriously. Don't take this wrong, but you're awfully pretty for a hardboiled detective type. I mean you're clearly good at this, based on how you dealt with those guys this morning, but you don't fit my image of the private dick with the cynical attitude and hardened face, scarred by one too many punches. How have you managed to keep yourself so unscathed?"

"Well, most bad guys aren't nearly as tough or as fast as they think they are. They've been bullies most of their lives and aren't used to dealing with people who actually know what they're doing. Nine times out of ten, they swing and miss, I land a solid shot, and they fold."

"Same with me. Most don't expect a girl who can hit like I do either."

"I imagine you pack a punch."

"I imagine you do too."

"I guess, but I've learned when to fight and when to pull a gun. I'm not more of a man if I outpunch the bad guy. Catching him is what counts and if I can save myself a broken nose in the process, I won't lose any sleep over having my tough guy card revoked."

"You're not…usual, are you?"

"I don't know what usual is, but probably not." Mannheim Steamroller's "Silent Night" came on. It was, and in my opinion still is, the best version of the song ever recorded. I love the little quiet breeze effect at the very end. It always evoked that quiet, cold night I envisage when I think of Christ's birth. "Anyway, how did you become a cop?"

"In my blood. Dad was NYPD. Moved here after he took a bullet in the back. He's okay but on permanent disability. My brother is still there. Just made detective. My family's pretty old school, though. No one expected me to go into the family business, least of all my mom. I love her more than anyone else on the planet, but she still believes there are boy jobs and girl jobs. Her dream for me was to be a teacher like her or, even better, a trophy wife."

"Not that you aren't trophy material, but that doesn't seem like you at all."

"It isn't. I wouldn't marry a man who would want me to stop—hold on a second. We've got company."

"Vehicle or on foot?"

"Black SUV, like the two you destroyed. Pulling in to the front of the Beauregard now. I'm going in."

I took the keys from the ignition, pulled my weapon from its holster on the passenger seat, and quickly exited the car, using care not to slam the door.

"Two. One's heading your way."

I sprinted for the storage shed at the back of the building. I saw muzzle flash instinctively ducked, which wouldn't have helped if his aim had been true, but it wasn't. He was probably surprised to see me and just fired from the hip. I dove into the corner where the shed and house met and rolled into shooting position. Trying hard to still my heart and silence my breathing, I listened for movement. Hearing none, I stole quietly toward the front corner of the building. When I reached it, I quickly peaked around the corner just as the first fat, cold drops of rain began to fall sporadically. I saw nothing, but just as my head was about to clear the corner, I glimpsed the very tip of the barrel of his gun appear. I squatted down, picked up a rock from the ground, hefted it in my hand a couple times, and then tossed it over the building, aiming for somewhere in the parking lot to the right of and beyond the shed. After a second there was a hollow thud as the baseball sized rock made impact with what sounded like the roof of a car. Crap. Mine was the only one there.

But the sound had its desired effect, as the gunsel turned and fired four times in rapid succession. By the time he had pulled the trigger for the fourth time I was on him. My hand came down hard on his wrist; a grunt preceded the sound of the gun crunching into the gravel beside the building. He was quick, though, because before I could get my gun on him, he grabbed my wrist with the other hand. We struggled for control of the weapon for a few seconds before he turned into me and drove his elbow into my face, smashing my nose. So much for unscathed. He must have expected me to go down, though, because he left himself open. I managed to stay upright and wrapped my free arm around his throat. We continued struggling with the gun for a few seconds, until he realized he was running out of air, at which time he let go of my gun hand and started clawing with both hands at the arm that was threatening to crush his larynx. I held on to my piece but used both arms to hold on to him until he quit kicking. He wasn't dead, but he wasn't likely to wake up for a bit.

I gathered both guns and was heading toward the front of the house in what was becoming a frigid downpour, when World War III broke loose. Having climbed the steps onto the wraparound porch, I flattened my back against the wall just around the corner from the front. In all, probably twelve shots were exchanged over no more than a ten-second period, followed by shocking silence. I stepped around, both guns drawn. There were two people on the porch; one was destined to assume room temperature. The other, Trooper Katelyn Todd, was wounded in the arm but otherwise appeared okay. As I reached her, the front door flew open. Silhouetted against the frame of the door, Dee stood, gun raised in front of her. When she saw us, she started to drop her gun to her side, but, before I realized what she was doing, she raised it again, firing three quick shots. Kate and I both turned, guns raised. A dead body slumped out of the back window, like the Escalade, riddled with bullet marks, had stuck its tongue out as it died. A pistol lay on the ground. A third man had been inside the SUV and was just about to shoot us both through the open window. I raised his head; Dee had put three bullets in a nearly perfect right triangle in the middle of his forehead. When I turned back, Dee was checking Kate's wounds. At some point, someone inside had turned on the porch light, so when Kate looked up she saw me clearly.

"Aw, no, Harry. You got scathed!"

Chapter 34

The rain fell steadily the rest of the night, but shortly before dawn, the clouds began breaking up in favor of what eventually became a spectacular sunrise. Muted grey and purple, deep as a bruise, softened into pastel pinks and violets as the light began to chase away the dark night, then finally gave way to brilliant yellow shafts that burst through the last of the rain clouds. It would have been breathtaking if I weren't sleep-deprived and jangly from entirely too much coffee.

The only saving grace was that the event had been trooper-involved, albeit an off duty trooper, and she was able to give a thorough account, so I was spared more than a single telling of my perspective, which was fine with me because, even though the EMTs found my nose wasn't broken, it still hurt like a mother and I was really getting tired of the guy playing the base drum inside my head. Kate was checked out, bandaged, and taken to the hospital in an ambulance. Procedure. It was a clean through-and-through, though, and the worst she was likely to expect was two scars, one in the middle of her left biceps and one toward the top of her triceps.

Mike Franks had shown up about 5:00am. By 7:00, Dee, he, and I were sitting in the parlor, I on about my thirtieth cup of coffee and he still on his first. To say that Dee was sitting is a bit of a stretch. Okay, it's purely fictive. She was stretched out on the couch, quietly snoring.

"Dead guy on the front porch," said Franks, "and the one you choked out were, again allegedly, mid-level operatives of Merton Bell. The live one's already lawyered up. The one that your wife took out was, interestingly enough, named Damon Werth, Merton Bell's right hand. Well, actually left hand. Former Marine. Lost his right arm in Afghanistan. Probably explains his sitting out the main action. You're moving up. Bell wouldn't send his top lackey unless he's mightily angered."

"Too bad it wasn't Bell himself." Dee's voice was muffled by the couch cushion. I guess she wasn't as asleep as I thought.

"What are you going to do about this?" asked Franks. "You can't just keep killing people and he's not likely to run out of hired guns any time soon."

"I was hoping," I said, "that if we fought off enough of them, Bell would see that we were too hard to kill and it was simply bad business to keep trying."

As we were talking, a crime scene tech knocked and entered. He was average height, just a shade under 6 feet, and thin except for a bit of dough around the middle. Beneath his hat was no hair at all. His scalp shone like it was freshly shaved and polished. Beneath his sleepy blue eyes (pretty much the only normal thing on his face) his nose was long, thin, and turned up at the end, a la Bob Hope. Seemingly stunted from lack of sunlight, his mouth was way too small. This was made even more pronounced by the fact of his anvil chin. It was like his mouth was the runt of the litter.

"Hey Lieutenant, telephone call." He handed Franks his cell.

"Who is it?"

"ME," The CSI's ID said his name was Gerald Jackson. I was half expecting it to say C. DeBergerac. "Said he has news and you need to take your phone off silent."

"Excuse me folks," Franks sighed as he heaved himself out of the chair and followed the tech out the door while putting the phone to his ear. As he did, Dee rolled over, sat up, mussed her hair with her left hand, and picked up her coffee cup with her right. Taking a sip, she grimaced and let out a shiver. She hated cold coffee. It never bothered me much as long as it was good coffee to begin with. Crappy coffee is crappy hot or cold. Good coffee is best hot but not worth throwing out if cold. It's a rule. This was good coffee, though I was about a half a pot past my tolerance. My tongue felt like a piece of jerky and I'm sure my breath would stop a buffalo in its tracks.

"What are we going to do Harry?" She poured her cold coffee in my mug before going to the table near the door to get a fresh cup. "Franks is right. We can't just keep running and fighting. We need an endgame."

Before I could answer, Franks walked in. I was glad because I was stumped. I had no idea what to do, short of going to Chicago and either trying to talk reason to Merton Bell or putting a bullet between his eyes. Neither choice seemed particularly appealing, but I was starting to think it was going to come down to one of the two. The question was what could I say to Bell to convince him to call off the assault? Or what could I give him? Even if Johnny gave up and went back, his life was over. You don't just turn your back on a mobster and then expect to live on just a sorry. And besides, who would want to go back? It didn't matter anyway. I'd do everything in my power not to let him.

"You bring a rifle with you?" asked Franks. Dee and I looked at each other, puzzled, and we both shook our heads. "Well, then, the plot thickens. They took five slugs out of the dead guy on the porch. Four Trooper Todd's, all center mass. But the kill shot hit him just above the right temple. Bullet zinged around his cranium playing Dig Dug with his brain. Came from above and to the left of Todd's position and from a pretty fair distance, 300 yards or more. ME says it was one hell of a shot."

Franks turned and walked outside; we rose to follow. From the front porch, it was clear there were only two possibilities. Bettie's Diner had relatively easy roof access to someone who knew what they were doing. It was directly dead ahead, though, and based on Kate's account, the shooter was facing straight toward her until he went down, so the shot likely came from the building a little further down the road.

"What's that building?" I pointed to the shabby two-story structure.

"Cliff and Claire's, an old mom and pop," said Franks. "Been closed for ten years. We'll check it out."

We all looked back and forth at each other as this new information sank in. There was another shooter. But who? Then it hit me. I smiled for the first time in hours.

"A ha, you son of a gun!" I shouted a little louder than I realized. Both of my companions, along with everyone within half a mile, jumped a little.

"What?" Dee asked.

"Who?" Franks asked.

"Bernhard Stultz."

"Really?" asked Dee. "I was afraid he was a goner."

"Who else could it be? There's absolutely no one else that even knows about this."

"Why does that name sound familiar?" Franks took his notebook from his pocket and started flipping through it.

"Probably came up in your investigation. Normally, he'd likely have led this latest raiding party. Glad he didn't. Would've ended badly."

"He's good?"

"He may be as good as Harry," said Dee. Sad but true.

"Well, based on this shot, I can hardly argue," said Franks. "It was pitch black with strong winds and heavy rain when he took it and he nailed the guy. He didn't fire twice."

"Not surprised," I said.

"What did you mean when you said 'normally'? He get religion or something?"

"Well, sort of. Remember I told you I had someone on the inside I was hoping could fix it? This is the guy. He was tasked with returning Johnny and Lilith to Bell. Between Dee's feminine wiles and my irresistible charm, we talked him into going back to Bell to try to convince him that he should let them go. That obviously didn't work out and we feared that Stultz had died in the attempt."

"So just like that he became a good guy?"

"It's more complex than that. He has rules. Not my rules and not what I'm sure your rules are, but rules nonetheless. He's kind of like Spenser's Hawk. He has no trouble killing people he feels deserve it, but he's not so willing if it violates his sense of fair play."

Franks nodded. He was like me, I could tell. He had rules that transcended the black-and-white of the law. That was obvious when he didn't arrest us yesterday.

"Borrow your phone, Lieutenant?"

"My friends just call me Mike," said Franks, handing me his cell. "You can call me Lieutenant. Your wife, on the other hand, can call me Mike all she wants."

"You're a smart man, Mike," said Dee, sitting in a rocking chair at the corner of the porch, looking quite satisfied.

I gave Dee a look as I punched in the number. I was going for contempt, but I think it came out more as indigestion. It rang twice.

"Hello?"

"Hey Bernhard. Glad you're not dead."

"As am I, Harry. More importantly, I'm quite relieved to see that your mesmerizing wife is none the worse for wear. I was terribly impressed by her shooting. But she looks quite cold. You would give her your coat if you were the man she thinks you to be."

I can't say that didn't startle me a little. As I put down the phone, took off my coat, wrapped it around Dee, and picked the phone back up, I scanned in every direction and saw no trace of him at first. But then I caught the briefest reflection off the lenses of his binoculars, powerful ones, based on how far away they appeared to be. I waved.

"Ah, guten. You found me."

"Yup. Come on in. We'll talk over breakfast."

"Lieutenant Franks might venture to arrest me. I would feel the need to resist. Police and I are a bad combination."

"The lieutenant's a little too forward with my wife, but not so bad otherwise."

"We can hardly blame him for that, can we? It's only a matter of time before she comes to her senses and realizes she can trade up rather easily. He and I are just jockeying for position for when the inevitable day comes."

"I'm confident the lieutenant won't arrest you. Less so that I won't shoot you."

"Now Harry, no need to be impetuous."

Chapter 35

Stultz arrived in a space gray metallic BMW Z4 convertible. It could have fit in the trunk of the Tankmobile and looked like a small rocket on wheels. Stultz, a large man, unfolded himself from the driver's seat with rather more agility than I expected, even from him. It reminded me of a one-man clown car.

"Couldn't find anything faster?" I held the door of Bettie's Diner open for him.

"Not legally," he replied.

"And that matters to you?"

"When it is convenient." I introduced Lieutenant Mike Franks. They eyed each other like two wolves circling before fighting.

"And you, of course, remember my wife." I said. I emphasized the my a little more than I probably should have. Not that I'm insecure. Stultz's demeanor changed immediately as he looked rather too long into her eyes before taking her hand in his, pulling it gracefully to his mouth, and kissing it.

"I would never forget you, mein fräulein."

"Frau to you, there, Bernhard," I said.

"Yes, yes." He waved his hands at me as if shooing away a pest. "I have missed you liebchen."

"Likewise, sweetie." She picked up her coffee cup with both hands and peeking over the rim. "Thanks for the assist. You saved my friend Kate. I owe you."

"I cannot wait to collect." They both knew this was driving me crazy, and both enjoyed it, for completely different reasons.

Before they could start necking, the waitress came to get our orders. I had the Denver Omelet, home fries, and a side order of fresh scratch-made biscuits with dark local honey that Bettie said was gathered by her nephew the beekeeper. Dee had a pancake with two pieces of turkey sausage and a fried egg over easy. Franks had biscuits and gravy with bacon and eggs over well. Stultz had a vegetable omelet without potatoes, no home fries, no biscuits, no toast, no carbs of any kind. His discipline irritated me sometimes. And by sometimes I mean only when he was in my presence—or anywhere else. I had hot tea—no coffee for me. The acid eating through my stomach lining was making me seriously consider never having coffee again. Dee had apple juice and water with lemon while Franks had coffee black and Stultz had hot tea with lemon.

"Good biscuits," I said. "Almost as good as my mom's."

"You should try 'em with the gravy," said Franks. "This would be my death row meal."

"May I please have a bite, Mike?" asked Dee, her smile on full power. She could have asked him to get up and kneecap me and he would've been powerless to say no. He cut off a bite and reached it across the table. She lipped it into her mouth, chewed for a few seconds and appeared to become borderline orgasmic.

"Omgawthasmazing!" she mumbled around what was apparently the best thing she'd ever eaten. Franks smiled with satisfaction like he had made the gravy himself.

"Things didn't go so well with Bell," I said to Stultz.

"Well, that is a bit of an odd story. I went to him with the intention of saying that we had lost Johnny and that we should give up the search because he would have gone to the police by now if he was going to and there was no way of knowing where he went anyway."

"You went with the intention of saying that?" asked Dee.

"Yes, but before I could finish what I had to say, his phone rang. When he looked at the screen, his eyes grew wide and he said he needed to take the call. A few minutes later, he came back into the room smiling and told me that it didn't matter because they knew they were in fact with you and where you were."

"They knew?" I said.

"Yes. He said you had stopped at a hotel outside Lexington and were planning to take the Bluegrass Parkway, where he would soon have operatives in place to intercept you. That was when I sent you the 911 text."

"Were we bugged?" asked Dee.

"We got rid of our cell phones," I said, "so they shouldn't have been able to trace us that way."

"A locater on Johnny's car?" asked Dee.

"They could know where you were," said Franks, "but how would they know where you were planning to go."

"Might have been a bug in their car," I said.

"Wouldn't a bug need a receiver somewhere nearby?" asked Dee.

"Hopefully that hole is plugged now," I said. "Bernhard, you know Bell. Suggestions?"

"Short of turning your friends over, all you can do is give him something he wants more than he wants to punish them."

"And that would be? Dee vocalized my exact thoughts.

"No idea, liebchen."

"Well thanks Bernhard," I said. "You've been a great help."

"I could have him arrested for attempted murder," said Franks.

"Wouldn't solve the problem," I said. "Bell could run his organization from the inside and the debt's still on the books."

"So we can't kill him, we can't arrest him, and until we know what he wants, we can't bargain with him," said Dee. "Then we're running again?"

"Well," I said, "we're in a different vehicle. There's a good chance that they won't know where we're going. Assuming it was the car and not one of us that was bugged. And assuming one of us isn't a rat. And assuming they aren't just following us with a spy plane or satellite." I needed sleep.

"Where are we going?"

"That's the beauty of it." I rose to pay the check. "We don't know either."

Chapter 36

The folks at the Beauregard Bed and Breakfast were kind enough to extend our check-out time. It was an easy offer to make since it was the end of the holiday weekend and we'd managed to scare away any of the paying customers they already had with our little Wild West show. Franks was heading to the hospital to check on Kate while Stultz, whose phone rang as he was walking out, just said he would be around, so after lingering for about twenty minutes just enjoying being quiet and alone together, Dee and I wandered hand in hand back to the Beauregard and headed up to the room with the intention of getting a quick nap before packing up to head for parts unknown. Unknown even to us. Before I could open the door, however, I was brought up short by what sounded like an argument inside the room.

"What's wrong?" asked Dee, a little too loudly.

"Shh! They're fighting."

I couldn't make out much of what was being said, and felt like it would be kind of bad form to stick my ear to the door, but Lilith was livid, though Johnny was being surprisingly quiet. So quiet I couldn't hear him. Maybe he was in the bathroom. Occasionally I caught a word or phrase, like "murdered," "shot," and "thought we had an understanding." The last one puzzled me a bit, but I've grown used to being puzzled over the years. It's such a constant state for me that it's almost disconcerting when I'm not.

We agreed it would be awkward to walk in on a fight, especially with her so wigged out, so we decided to crash in the parlor for a bit.

"Quiet," said Dee, who went in before me. "You'll wake Johnny."

"Huh? Who?"

"Johnny. Wait! Huh?" Johnny was slumped on the far end of the couch with his head lulled back on the wood trim at the top of the couch and his mouth gaping open. A gentle snore occasionally punctuated his deep, relaxed breathing. A half-eaten cherry Danish and cold cup of coffee sat on the table in front of him, while a wadded paper napkin had apparently fallen from his hand onto the floor at his right foot. We looked at each other, at Johnny, and then all around the room. "What?" Dee alternated between pointing at Johnny and up the stairs toward the room.

"Is there a secret passage?" I asked.

"Maybe behind a book shelf?"

"Passage to what," said Johnny, awakened by our talking but still quite groggy. He smacked his lips sleepily, squinted, rubbed the backs of his fists over his eyes, and shook his head softly.

"Your wife talk to herself?" I sat next to him as Dee sat on the chair across from us. She kicked off her brown suede clogs, pulled her legs up onto the chair, rested her stockinged feet on the edge of the chair, and hugged her knees. "More specifically, does she ever get in heated arguments with herself?"

Johnny looked at me like I had lobsters coming out of my ears. "No. I do. No fights. Not heated ones, anyway. Why?"

"We just came from upstairs," said Dee, "and didn't go into the room because we heard Lilith having a big wingding. We thought it was with you, but now, not so much."

He looked back and forth between the two of us, running his hand through his disheveled hair. "This a joke? If so, it isn't funny. Doesn't even make sense."

"No joke," Dee said, dropping her feet onto the tops of her clogs and leaning toward Johnny. "She was really chewing someone a new one. If not you, who?"

Johnny squinted at the Danish and ran his open right hand over his chin for a few seconds, then squeezed his mouth together on the sides with his thumb and index finger. This made what I'm sure he did not intend to be a funny fish face. Letting go of his face, he raised both hands to his sides, palms up and shrugged his shoulders.

"Maybe she was on the phone?" he asked.

That would explain why we only heard her half of the conversation, but to whom could she have been speaking? I told him what we had heard and as I was saying them, something started to dawn on me. Several things that had nagged at me were falling into place. I looked at Dee, whose eyes and mouth grew wide. "No! Really?"

"What?" asked Johnny.

"I think so," I said.

"Would you two please stop talking in riddles?"

"Who would she have an understanding with?" I asked.

"Haven't the faintest notion." He shook his head slowly.

"Maybe Merton Bell?" asked Dee.

"MERTON BELL!" he shouted. He took it better than I thought he would, actually. "What in God's name is that supposed to mean?"

"Well," I replied. "So many things have been odd. Taken by themselves they didn't mean much, but put together, they're significant."

Johnny's face became crimson. He rubbed the fingertips of both hands up and down on his forehead. "What things?"

"She argued to go back to Bell when we first left. I initially thought she just didn't believe what we were saying. But then, after the Bluegrass Parkway, her response was unusual. She said, 'I was almost killed.' Not we, not you. I. Like she thought she was supposed to be safe for some reason."

"And she came to our room," said Dee, "before we left that day. Harry was getting my drink. She asked where we were going and then left immediately. Meant nothing then, but Stultz said Bell got a phone call at what turns out to be the same time. Announced that he knew where we were going, prompting Stultz's nine-one-one."

"And then at the fast food restaurant," I continued. She's agitated; keeps repeating that she can't believe it. Goes to the bathroom comes back calm, like she's had her fears allayed."

"And," said Dee, "who else could she have an understanding with, if it's not you, Johnny?"

He had listened quietly until now, but suddenly bolted from his seat, his hands balled into tight fists at his sides. His breath was ragged and raspy as tears spilled from the corners of his eyes and down his cheeks. He began pounding his fists into his thighs, and his mouth moved silently for a few seconds like someone had hit his mute button, but he eventually found his voice.

"Oh God, I was afraid of this!" His voice was harsh and strangled. "I've been afraid for so long, but when she left with me, I finally hoped I'd been wrong. How could she do this to me?"

"Afraid of what Johnny?" Dee asked. I imagine she and I both knew what he was afraid of, but it had to be asked.

"I had suspected something was going on with her and Bell," he said after gathering himself for a minute. "I told myself it was just my imagination, but deep down I think I knew. The way they looked at each other. How much time they seemed to spend together for no apparent reason. And then she tried to talk me into going back every time we were alone together. She kept telling me that she just knew that, 'Merton will forgive you, Merton will take us back.'"

I rose from my seat. The others followed my lead and a few seconds later, we were outside the door

Sliding in his key card and turning the knob, Johnny opened the door wide and we all looked in, but Lilith was nowhere in sight. "Lil?" Johnny called out. No answer. I crossed to the bathroom and looked in. The shower curtain was open. As I stepped out, Johnny was closing the closet door as Dee stood up after looking under the bed. Finally, just to be sure, I stepped out onto the balcony. Nothing. I went to the railing and looked around. She wasn't anywhere out front. We wandered around the upstairs calling out for her, but to no avail.

We went out and back down the stairs. Cadet Lee was manning the desk, but reported that he'd seen no one come or go other than the three of us. "Though I may be mistaken." That was helpful. Guess he'd started the Irish coffee early this morning. We headed out the front door, pausing to look around. She wasn't sitting on the porch. I was starting to get a weird feeling in the pit of my stomach.

"You guys go around that way," I said, pointing to the right, "and I'll go around the other way and check the trail out into the woods. We'll meet back here in five minutes."

We went our separate ways. I started out walking, but at some point, without realizing I had started, I found myself jogging as I reached the tree line. At first, I could hear Dee and Johnny occasionally shout Lilith's name, but within a minute or two, I was out of earshot. The path wound through the woods and away from the inn. I too shouted Lilith's name from time to time, but after a few minutes, I started to lose hope of locating her. I was several years younger than she, about a foot taller, and was a pretty fast runner. If I hadn't caught up to her by now, she wasn't on this trail. After approximately another minute, I stopped and turned, walking to catch my breath. I looked all around and continued to call her name, but the woods were without undergrowth for the most part. It had been cleared and had an almost park-like air to it. Having caught my breath, I kicked back into a jog, almost a run. I was met at the edge of the woods by Johnny and Dee.

"Anything?" asked Dee.

"No sign of her. Unless she's a lot faster runner than I think she is she didn't come this way. You?"

"Could she have walked to the diner?" asked Johnny desperately.

It was the last place we hadn't looked. I didn't feel like she'd had time to make it there in the short time we'd been in the parlor, but I didn't know it and we needed to check before we called out the cavalry. Oh yes, that's her officer. Sorry we forgot to look in the most obvious place.

By this time, we had made it back to the front of the Beauregard, so it was quicker to get there on foot than by car. It was late morning, so the place was pretty much deserted, other than two retirement age men, one white and one black, at the far end of the bar drinking coffee and arguing without much enthusiasm about something in the newspaper between them. Bettie was restocking napkin dispensers and condiment bottles behind the bar as a waitress was doing the same at the tables. The line cook, a large bald man with the bottom of a tattoo that may have been a mermaid or may have been a fish sticking out from the right sleeve of his white t-shirt, was scraping down the flat top.

"Hey folks!" said Bettie enthusiastically. The woman's energy, if they could find a way to collect it, would light up a small town. "Sorry, you just missed the others."

Uh oh.

"Others?" Dee asked.

"Yeah, Mrs. Tuttle and that pretty German just pulled out. Seemed like they were in a bit of a hurry. He didn't even come in. Just pulled up in that rocket ship and she ran out and they were gone."

"Did she say anything?" I asked.

"Naw, just stood by the door, all out of breath. Asked if I could get her anything. Just shook her head and 'bout that time he came a'roaring into the parking lot."

"He kidnapped her!" shouted Johnny.

"So she left voluntarily?" I asked.

"Sure seemed that way. Like I said, he never even got out."

"Johnny," said Dee, "She came here to meet him. He didn't kidnap her. He picked her up."

"But, but, why?" We all knew the answer. Even Johnny had to know. It seemed obvious that she was on her way back to Bell of her own volition. Johnny collapsed into the bench seat of the booth behind him and held his head in his hands with his elbows propped on his knees. If the booth hadn't been there, he may well have simply folded onto the floor. His hands were clinched in his hair so tightly that I was genuinely concerned he was going to start ripping it out. All the color had drained from his face and his eyes were wide as if he were watching some horrible goblin rising up out of the floor toward him. He had clearly reached his breaking point. For what seemed like the fiftieth time that day, Dee and I looked at each other, completely at a loss. I like to think I'm a relatively bright guy, but I would have to admit that, though I was starting to suspect that Lilith was up to something, I certainly did not see this coming.

I asked Bettie if I could borrow her phone. She handed me a wireless handset and I dialed Stultz' number. Straight to voicemail. I tried again, though I have no idea what made me think it would work. It didn't. I started to leave a message, but what was I going to say? I handed Bettie the phone back and sat down on the booth bench beside Dee. I was suddenly exhausted. Not just physically, but tired in my heart, tired in my soul.

"What do we do now?" asked Dee.

As if being powered by some invisible power outside himself, Johnny rose up, hollow-eyed, zombie-like and walked out the door with Dee and me just watching, dumbfounded. Having no idea what else to do, we got up and followed him.

"John." I came abreast of my friend. "Where we going?"

"Chicago." His voice was without inflection, his face flat and completely without expression.

"Then what?" Dee asked, finally catching up to the two of us.

"Get Lilith. Kill Bell." He said it so matter-of-factly that he may have been reading a phone book.

"Wait, Johnny," said Dee, "let's talk about this."

"Talk about what? Can't get her back, don't want to live. Don't want Bell to live."

"Okay," I said, "but you can't just walk into his house and kill the guy. You'll be dead before you even see him. Or Lilith for that matter."

This gave him pause. He stopped, looked at the two of us, and slowly nodded his head.

"You'll come with me?"

"How about I go instead of you?" I asked.

"No, this is my problem." His face was still without affect, except his eyes grew wide and wild. "Want him to see my face as he's dying. All those years his prisoner and now he's taken the one joy I had left. He has to pay. And I'm going to collect."

Chapter 37

It was only when we returned to the room and began to pack up that we realized that Lilith had not only bolted without taking any luggage with her, but she had also left her purse behind. Johnny looked at it for a long time like it was a giant spider about to attack him, but eventually picked it up and looked inside. His eyes widened as he reached inside, pulling out a cell.

"She told me she threw this away way back in Marietta," he said.

"Now we know how Bell kept up with us. May I see?"

He looked at me sort of blank for a few seconds as if I was speaking a language he didn't understand, but eventually handed me the phone. I went through the call history, and, sure enough, there were several calls to Merton Bell's private number. I knew this because it was listed as, "Merton's Private #." Subtle. The next to last call coincided with the time we heard her arguing in the room. She was yelling at Bell. I guess the understanding was that she wasn't supposed to be in the line of fire. The last call, however, I recognized as being to Bernhard Stultz. I hit redial. The number rang this time.

"Hello Harry."

"Bernhard, I'm disappointed. I thought I could trust you and you turn out to be a double agent."

"Oh, Harry, on the contrary." He laughed. "I made a rhyme."

"Yes, yes you did." This guy was more easily amused than I am. "Anyway, why did you take Lilith?"

"I did not take her. I fetched her at her request. As you can no doubt see from the call history on her phone, she called me. Bell assures me that, assuming Frau Tuttle is returned unharmed, all will be forgiven. Herr Tuttle is a free man, in every sense of the word. Free of Bell and free of his wife."

"That's lovely, Bernhard, except Johnny doesn't want to be free of Lilith. He wants her back and he wants to kill Bell."

Johnny ripped the phone from my hand before I could protest. "Stultz, I want to speak to my wife immediately—Lilith, honey, what are you doing? But you're my wife, you're all that matters to me in the world—you can't—no, I won't let you—I know if you'll just listen to me, we can work things out."

He took the phone from his ear and looked at the screen, puzzled, hoping the battery had died or they'd lost connection and not that she'd hung up on him. Then he calmly walked out onto the balcony. We both followed, worried he may pitch himself off and do a face plant in the front parking lot. Instead, he stood with his hands on the gleaming white rails for maybe two minutes before raring back to fire the phone into the distance. I grabbed his arm.

"What? Why?"

"This is our only working cell. And besides, it may have numbers we need."

We were packed, paid up, and back on the Bluegrass Parkway within a half hour, this time headed north. It was nearly noon, and I figured it was probably going to take us about 8 hours to get to the outskirts of Chicago, so we agreed that we would stop just south of there and get a hotel so we could be rested for the big event. I wasn't sure what else to call it. It certainly wasn't a party. It was a reunion of sorts, but not in the oh-wow-it's-so-great-to-see-you-again-I've-missed-you-so-much sense. It was more the give-my-wife-back-and-eat-hot-death sort of soirée.

I advised Dee to climb in the back and get a nap in case the adrenaline wore off and I needed spelled on the driving duties. She didn't argue. In fact, she dove in almost before I got the words out of my mouth and was asleep before we hit the Parkway. Between her diminutive size and the sheer magnitude of the back seat, she didn't even need to curl up.

I don't know how long Johnny was silent. I fiddled with the radio, trying to find a radio station I could stand. The station I'd been listening to must have been too weak and too distant to be heard from our location during the day. I eventually gave up, pulled my mp3 player from my pocket, and plugged the USB cable into the receptacle on the bottom left of the stereo's face plate. After a few seconds, the stereo recognized my player and a menu popped up on the digital display to allow me to scroll through my playlists. I chose Michael Bublé. "Feelin' Good" came on; I sang along under my breath.

"What are we going to do?" Johnny finally asked.

"Well, I thought we might actually just walk into Mordor," I said. "But not before making a call to make sure Sauron is home, so to speak, and willing to give us an audience. No use in fighting your way in if you can just walk in all peaceful-like."

"But what if Sauron, er, Bell says no?"

"I'm pretty persuasive. And he'll talk to us when he finds out that you have gathered up enough evidence on him over the years to put him away for several lifetimes."

"But I don't have any evidence."

"He doesn't know that."

"But can't he just shoot us when we get there?"

"Not if we explain that the evidence is in a safe place with instructions that, if something happens to us or we aren't heard from immediately, it is to be taken to a certain detective I know named Otis Campbell in Parkersburg, WV. If you're going to lie, do it boldly and do it in great detail."

"I'll try to remember that next time I'm in a life-or-death situation."

"Johnny, what you need to remember is to stay out of life-or-death situations."

"Thanks for the tip."

"In all seriousness, you need to consider what you're going to do when you talk to Lilith if she really doesn't want to leave with you."

"That's not going to happen."

"But what if it does?"

"IT WON'T!"

"Okay, calm down. I'm not trying to be mean or anything, but she left on her own and didn't mind people slinging lead at you as long as she wasn't going to have to catch any of it."

"She's just not thinking straight. We've been married for almost thirty years. I know she loves me. I just need to remind her."

I left it at that. Nothing I could say was going to help at this point. I just had to hope that he would eventually think it through and allow his head to overcome his heart. Otherwise, things were going to get messy. When Dee woke up, she asked if I wanted her to take a turn, which I did. After a gas and a potty break, she took the wheel and I took the back seat, which was roomy, even for my bulky frame. I was sleepy, but I wanted to do some things before I tried, almost certainly in vain, to nap. I don't sleep in cars. I'm certain no one can drive safely unless I'm awake. What control issues?

Anyway, using Lilith's phone, I found a Motel 6 in Merrillville,

Indiana, just south of Chicago. I told Dee of our destination for the

night and, to my surprise, fell almost immediately into a deep sleep.

The next thing I knew, I was standing in Merton Bell's

house. I had no idea how I knew it was his house, because it didn't

even resemble what little description I'd heard from Johnny. I just

knew. There was no one around, but there was blood everywhere,

flowing through hallways like rivers and down a stairway like a

many-tiered waterfall of gore. I didn't want to follow it, but I did,

like an explorer searching for the source of a river. I climbed the

steps, trying to avoid the horrible liquid, but it splashed all over me

until it had soaked into my clothes and was dripping off me in long

rivulets. I could smell it and taste the harsh metallic flavor in my

mouth. At the top of the stairs, at the end of a long hallway, was a

door that seemed to stay just as far away no matter how long I

walked. I tried to run, but it was like the blood was clotting around

me, making me almost incapable of moving. After what seemed like

an hour, I finally made it to the entrance. I knew what was inside that

door was something I didn't want to see, but something was

impelling me forward. I stuck my head around the corner and my eyes were met with a sight so gruesome it defies full description. Bodies littered the room; all were riddled with bullets and each bullet hole gushed blood unendingly. Some faces I knew; others were strangers. There was Johnny Tuttle; over there was Lilith. I saw Hagrid and General Robert E. Lee—the real one, not the owner of the Beauregard. All had their eyes wide open in shock, as if they were taken by surprise by their grisly end. Something told me that I had to turn around. I fought it with every fiber of my being, but some outside force wrestled against me with equal strength. Eventually, my energy ebbed, and the force won. As I spun around, I saw it. She was beautiful, aside from where the blood burbled out like so many underground springs. I knew that body like I knew my own. I recognized the pale pink polish on the toes and fingers, the soft curve of her calf, the scar where she had fallen off of a swing as a little girl and gashed a huge chunk out of her knee. Her arms were crossed over her chest, as if, even in death, she felt modesty. Finally, I looked into those beautiful chocolate eyes, now dulled, and at her copper hair, now smeared with blood, which, instead of clotting, was running out and oozing from the ends of her hairs like they could somehow bleed too. In the middle of her porcelain forehead, a bullet-hole poured forth an eternal fountain of red. I heard a horrified

scream that started out as a strangled bark, but grew until it was loud

and shrill to the point of deafening me. I tried to lift my hands to my

ears, but my arms refused to move.

As I started to awaken, I realized the screaming was coming

from me. I struggled to climb out of the dark abyss of this ghastly

nightmare and couldn't understand why I could still taste the blood.

As I slowly came back to the world of the living, I realized I'd been

chewing on my tongue. Fully awake, it took me a few seconds to

make sense of the huge, bright white 6 I saw staring down at me and

of the panicked voices I heard asking me if I was okay. I sat up

quickly and wrapped my arms around my wife, who was

inexplicably now sitting beside me, so relieved she was still alive

that I couldn't stop the tears that poured out of my eyes.

Chapter 38

It took us all a few minutes to calm down. Johnny and Dee inferred that I had had a nightmare, but I refused to tell about it. I just said I didn't remember it except that something was chasing me. No need to worry anyone else. I don't believe in omens, but if I did, that seemed to qualify.

I checked us in to two rooms with my credit card. No need to try to hide anymore. By the time they knew we were here, it was all going to be over with, one way or the other, anyway. As soon as we hit the room, Dee went straight to the bathroom. I could hear the shower running as I scrolled through the call history on the cell and found the number. Hitting send, I waited through three rings before hearing the click of the call connecting.

"Hello, sugar lumps," said a man I presumed to be Bell in a syrupy, almost baby-like, voice. "Are you almost here?"

"Hi there, sweet-cheeks. Yes, we are quite nearby, though I have a sneaking suspicion you meant that for someone else. I figured Lilith and Bernhard would have been there by now."

"Who is this?"

"I imagine you can probably guess, but I'll save you the time. This is Harry Shalan and I have Johnny Tuttle with me. He wants to see you, but more importantly, he wants to talk to his wife."

"You're nuts."

"So I'm told, but you may find it interesting that Johnny didn't just randomly decide to run one day. He has enough evidence to bring your entire organization down—names, dates, payoffs to cops, who is on your payroll, which games were thrown and by whom, even where the bodies are buried—and he brought it to me. It's with someone I trust who has instructions to take that information directly to a detective friend of mine named Otis Campbell if he or she doesn't hear that I've met with you and am safely on my way home."

"Why didn't he just take it to the cops to begin with?" asked Bell. A fair question. Think Shalan, think.

"He didn't want the trouble. He just wants to be left alone. That would've been enough right up until he found out you've been boinking his wife. What he would like to do now is put a bullet in your brain, but mostly he wants Lilith back and is willing to let it go at that as long as you are amenable."

"How do I know you're not lying?"

"You don't. You and I both know you can't take the chance, though."

There was a long pause, during which I could almost hear him thinking.

"My house tomorrow, 9:00am."

The shower was still running, so I stepped next door to tell Johnny the news. He was clearly nervous, but seemed relieved that we were going to finally get this issue resolved, good or bad. Or maybe I was just projecting.

Upon returning to my room, I found Dee at the sink drying her hair in her birthday suit. I kissed her neck gently before starting to disrobe for my own shower.

"Johnny and I are going to Bell's house at nine tomorrow morning," I said, turning on the faucet, hopeful that she hadn't used all the hot water in the entire building.

"What do you mean Johnny and you?" she asked. I knew I wasn't going to slip it past her, but took a shot anyway.

"I'm hoping we're just going to talk, but we need someone to stay with the car in case it doesn't go as well as it could and we have to perform a tactical withdrawal."

"Bull."

"Okay, and I just can't stand the thought of putting you in harm's way yet again. I know walking in there that I may have to shoot my way out."

"All the more reason you need me." She held the hair dryer like a weapon at her side. "Johnny is just an English teacher."

"I used to just be an English teacher, just like Johnny."

"You were never just like Johnny. You've been shooting guns all your life and could take care of yourself in a fight before you did it for a living. You've done martial arts forever. He really is just a teacher. You need me and you know it."

I hated it when she was right, especially about something like this. I simply couldn't argue with her. Our chances of survival improved astronomically if she was standing beside me, no matter how violently opposed I was to the idea. My heart screamed no almost loudly enough to drown out my mind saying that it had to be. And either she was going to be my partner or she wasn't. I couldn't keep her safe all the time. Just being married to me was a risk, so it

may as well be a risk she faced with her eyes open and gun drawn.

Fully disrobed, I pulled her to me and wrapped her in a long

embrace, comforted by the feeling of her warm skin pressed against

mine. She wrapped her slender but strong arms around my waist and

squeezed back. Eventually, I let her go and went to take my shower.

"Wow, either I'm slipping or you must really be a wreck.

Naked hug and you didn't even try anything."

"Trust me, babydoll, you aren't slipping," I said as I climbed

in the shower. It occurred to me as I let the hot water wash over me

that, if the unthinkable happened the next day, this could be our last

night together. I don't know if she was thinking the same thing or if

she just wanted reassurance that she really wasn't slipping, but after

a few seconds, I heard the dryer click back off and the curtain

rustling as she climbed into the shower behind me, again wrapping

her arms around me. I turned and kissed her, tentatively at first, but it

quickly grew in ardor. Her passion was almost tangible, causing all

thoughts of anything but becoming one with this ferociously

beautiful woman immediately dissolved and ran down the drain with

the water.

Completely spent from our extended shower, we climbed out and affectionately towel-dried each other. I held the blow dryer as she combed through her hair with her fingers until it was sufficiently dry for us to climb into bed, where we were both out cold in a matter of a few minutes. I'm happy to report that my sleep was free of nightmares. I did dream, but nothing I can share in polite company.

Chapter 39

The motel had no fitness facilities, so I opted for a short run when I woke up at 6:00AM. There was a mall a couple blocks east, so I ran over there and around the perimeter of the parking lot a couple times before heading back. Dee was still dead asleep when I slipped in. Working as quietly as I could, I made the in-room coffee and jumped in the shower. Using almost completely cold water in the hopes of cooling off enough not to come out of the shower sweating after my run, I was definitely awake by the time I got finished. The coffee was finished, so I poured a cup before shaving.

"Ugh, what time is it?" Dee mumbled sleepily from somewhere under the covers.

"Seven-thirty-five," I said. "Time to get up. Big day ahead. Hate to have a gunfight on an empty stomach."

I finished shaving and packed up my toiletry kit, tossing it on my side of the bed. I poured her a cup of coffee, placed it on the stand beside her, and yanked the blankets back, revealing her naked body. She must really have been tired last night, because she never sleeps in the nude. She yanked the blankets back up, shouting something unintelligible, though I caught a snippet about cutting something off. After a few minutes, though, she was sitting up on the side of the bed with the blankets wrapped around her, sipping her coffee, which she held in both hands.

As I dressed and packed, she got up, stretched, and began the process of getting prepared for the day. Once I was packed, I took my luggage to the car and knocked on Johnny's door on the way back to the room. He answered much more quickly than I expected. He was fully dressed with his luggage packed and sitting on the bed, which he had either made or hadn't slept in. Based on the almost bruised-looking purple-gray bags under his pronouncedly bloodshot eyes, I was more apt to guess the latter. "You okay?"

"Fine. Ready to go?"

"Nearly. Just waiting on Dee to finish up. You want to take you stuff to the car? I can give you a hand."

"No, just give me the keys, please. I can do it."

I handed him the keys and stepped the few feet over to our room, using the key card to unlock the door. Dee was nearly dressed and nearly finished packing when I arrived.

"Check the shower, will you sweetie?" she requested when she saw me.

I pulled back the curtain, found nothing that belonged to us, and reported same, so she closed up her toiletry bag and packed it in her largest suitcase. Giving one last look around, she nodded, apparently satisfied we hadn't forgotten anything, and closed up the bag. I picked up everything but her purse, which she grabbed and then opened the door for me. I was pretty much on auto pilot, walking to where I knew the car to be. Unfortunately, when I got to the spot, that's all there was—an empty spot. I looked all around, hoping I was mistaken, but knew I wasn't. Crap.

"What's wrong? Oh, the car! Where is it?"

"I gave the keys to Johnny so he could pack his luggage. He must have taken it."

"But why?"

"I guess he wanted to deal with Bell without us."

"But that's insane!"

"I know that and you know that, but I am guessing that he either doesn't know that or doesn't care."

"Oh no!" Dee shouted.

"What?" I asked.

"I left your spare piece in the glove box. Johnny saw me put it in there. He has a gun."

This morning was getting better and better. I ran to the front desk, checked out, and asked the clerk to please call me a cab as quickly as possible, that it was an extreme emergency. She was on the phone as I went back out to join Dee. Because Merrillville is a relatively small place or just through sheer dumb luck, a cab arrived in less than five minutes. The driver popped the trunk and we dumped our luggage inside before piling into the back seat.

"Where to folks?" he asked. He reminded me of John Candy. His badge, hanging on the dash, told me he was Russell Buck. No, I'm not kidding.

"You know how to get to North Shore? Locust Road?"

"Yeah I do, but that's forever from here. It'll cost you a small fortune," he said.

"I know," I said, "but we're in a hurry. This is literally a life-and-death situation. There's an extra hundred in it for you if you pretend there are no traffic laws or speed limits."

He apparently needed to hear nothing more, as he laid a patch of rubber pulling away. I calculated in my head that it should take us around an hour and a half to get there driving normally, but this guy was not driving normally. He weaved in and out of morning rush hour traffic like he was late to defuse a nuclear bomb. He passed on the shoulder, in the median, anywhere that had enough space to get through. He did most of this with one hand because he was busy honking the horn and gesturing with the other. Lots of people in the Chicago metro area were number one this morning. By the time we got there, I was pretty sure I'd wet myself and had to resist the urge to dive out and kiss the ground. When he hit Locust Road, I asked him to slow down so we could look for our car because I didn't know the exact address. It only took about two minutes to find, so we climbed out on unsteady legs, retrieved our luggage, and I went to pay the fare.

"Nah, forget it," he said. "I've wanted to do that all my life. It was worth every penny." And with that, he was gone.

The car was left where it had busted through the gate. We piled our luggage behind it and checked our firepower. I pulled a spare piece I'd acquired from Katelyn Todd from my bag, along with extra bullets, and handed them to Dee. It was only a .32, but we weren't going to be trying to take down any bear that day or, I hoped, firing from any distance. Most gunfights are much more intimate than people think. This gun would stop an adult from 25 feet or so, but most often, I've found myself shooting at people from well inside that range. My real goal was not to have any shots fired at all, but Johnny getting the jump on us brought the odds of that down to nearly zero. She checked her clip and stowed four spares in her coat pocket. I was packing my usual, a Bersa .9mm. I had decided to leave the howitzer at home.

As armed as we were going to get, we approached the gate with caution. We needn't have bothered, though, as we discovered the body of one of Bell's men lying across the driveway with a bullet hole in his forehead. To my great relief, there was no geyser of blood coming out of it. Dee's spare gun was a revolver, and the guard's piece was still beside him, so Johnny had five shots left before he would have to reload. I wasn't sure he even knew how to do that, but before a few seconds ago, I wouldn't have guessed he could outgun a professional thug.

We stayed along the ten-foot tall hedges on the right hand side of the drive, jogging the quarter mile to the large circle in front of the house. All was quiet. Disquietingly quiet. When close enough, I could see that the front door was ajar. We faced about 75 feet of open ground between us and the door, but we didn't have time to decide if it was safe.

"Stay as close behind me as you can without running up my back." Dee nodded. Holding my gun to my side and out away from me a bit, I bolted out of the cover of the hedge and toward the house, Dee almost literally at my heel. No one fired on us or yelled at us or even noticed us, as far as I could tell. I wasn't sure if I was relieved or worried.

I didn't have much time to think about it, though. We had planted our backs on either side of the door, I at the hinge side, so I reached over with my right hand and pushed it open. The response was almost instantaneous. I had no idea what the person was shooting, but it sounded like a blunderbuss. It hit high, placing several dents in the reinforced door. Buck shot. I got down on my belly and peeked around the door frame quickly, hoping the shooter was looking higher. He wasn't looking higher. He wasn't looking anywhere. I waited a few seconds and then looked around more slowly to confirm what I thought I saw. He was dead or unconscious. We got his last shot before he bled out. Two bullet holes stained his white button-down shirt. One was in the gut, another in the right upper chest. A sawed off double-barreled 12-gauge shotgun lay at his side. Old school. Johnny had three bullets left. A trail of bloody partial footprints led past the dual staircases and down a wide corridor to a double door that, based on Johnny's description, should lead to the veranda and gigantic back yard. Both doors were wide open; there was blood smeared on the facing. It seemed way too plentiful to belong only to this guy, which was extremely worrisome.

"Too much blood." Dee said what I was thinking. "Johnny's been hit."

Staying low, we darted the sixty feet past the large, wide staircases and down the corridor. A bloody handprint smeared down the glass of the door. If Johnny was still alive, he wasn't going to be for long. We had to hurry. But we would be no help to him if we got shot, so we couldn't just barrel through the door.

Crouching behind a large potted palm just inside the door, I looked outside. Johnny was out of sight, but Merton Bell and Lilith stood just beyond an overturned table. She didn't appear to be

injured, but she was definitely not happy, as Bell was standing

behind her, his left arm wrapped around her throat and his right hand

holding a gun to her head. I had a feeling that Lilith's feelings for

Bell might be changing. I couldn't see anyone else around, so we

both stepped out the door, guns raised. Johnny stood twenty feet

away from Bell. Well, standing is probably too strong a word. He

was leaning against the back of a white wrought iron chair, clearly

weakened by blood loss. But the gun was steady.

"Merton, please, why are you doing this?"

"Shut up Lilith!"

"But you love me. You killed that horrible man Bloom for

me!"

"I didn't do it for you, you moron! He was a pain in my ass.

He couldn't quit bragging about how he was my right hand man.

And then he starts telling people how he and his buddy Rutger were

nailing you in your own house. He was dead anyway, but making

you think I did it for you sure made your pants fly right off."

"Shut up Bell!" screamed Johnny, seemingly reinvigorated by rage at hearing so graphically of his wife's infidelity. "I will blow your brains out!"

"Go ahead and shoot, big man. You'll only drill your slut of a wife. Might as well—everybody else has."

I felt certain I had to step in or Johnny was going to snap and kill his own wife. It had to crush him to hear just how much of a stranger his wife had turned out to be. This woman, his angel as he always called her, turned out to be Bell and his men's willing plaything.

"It takes a big man to hide behind a woman, Bell," I said. He was startled enough to lose his grip on Lilith, who immediately crumpled to the ground. Bell turned his weapon toward us, but Dee and I both fired three times before he could pull the trigger. All six shots hit home. He pitched backwards like a felled tree to the concrete patio. His head bounced hard, making the sound of a watermelon breaking open after being dropped off a table. A blood pool quickly grew behind his head. I started toward him, but before I could make it two steps, I heard a crack and felt a searing pain in my right shoulder. This was followed by three more shots, from a different, larger gun, though I didn't feel the impact of those. I dropped to a knee and pivoted to my right, holding my gun up in my dominant left hand. I was thankful for once for being left-handed.

To my right, I saw Dee, gun pointed at Lilith, who was mortally wounded. Bell's gun, which he dropped as he was falling, fell into her lap. I guess I was wrong about her feelings changing. She had grabbed up the gun and fired in my general direction. From that distance, less than ten feet, she could hardly miss. I was lucky she didn't blow my brains out the back of my head. Before she could shoot again, though, Dee put three into her chest. I was beginning to feel like I would have to admit she was a better shot than I, but before I could ruminate on it, Johnny pulled one more trick out of his bag of crazy.

"Lilith—no!" he screamed, turning his gun on Dee. There was murder in his eyes, but he hesitated for just a moment, giving me time to bolt from my knee and dive in front of Dee, firing at Johnny twice as I saw three bright flames leave the barrel of his gun in quick succession. Then all I saw was red. I felt new pain, like a white-hot branding iron being driven into my chest. As I fell into a deep, dark pit of silence, the last thing I heard was Dee scream my

name and the report of her gun going off.

Chapter 40

I felt no pain at all. In fact, I felt nothing but pure contentment. I could see everyone around me, but it was like I was watching through a mist—a mist of unadulterated joy. I looked down to make sure my body was still there. Flexing my fingers and moving my arms and legs proved everything worked, but it was almost like operating an automaton by remote control, because things moved when I thought about them, but I felt nothing.

Suddenly, the mist formed a kind of tunnel. On the far end of the tunnel was a Light, brighter than any I'd ever seen, brighter even than the sun, though I found I could look directly at it without having to squint or shade my eyes. It felt warm, but not on my skin. It was like it warmed me from the inside out. The warmth was more emotional than physical, as if the Light was entirely made of affection. I had an overwhelming desire to walk to that Light, so I told my remote control body to start moving, which it did. But before I could get far, I heard a voice cry out. Not just any voice— Dee's voice. I told my head to turn, so I could see why she was crying. I couldn't imagine why anyone would have any reason to be sad under these circumstances. Far off, I could see her, kneeling over what appeared to be a body. Whose body? I walked closer, intending to just yell for her to follow me to the Light.

As I approached, I realized it was my body. But that made no sense—I was standing there, in my body, watching her kneel over my body. Then I remembered something. I got shot. *Oh*, I thought, *I'm dead*. I wasn't upset. The thought occurred to me much like it would occur to me that I was hungry or sleepy. It was just a fact. Actually, the more I thought about it, the more I liked the idea. But Dee seemed so sad. Her tortured sobs broke my heart. More than I wanted to go into the Light, I wanted to be with my Dee and make her happy again. I looked back at the Light and felt it give me permission to go back.

The next thing I remembered was waking up in a hospital bed. I was on a respirator and felt like a human pin-cushion. All around me were the sounds of the machines but my eyes felt like they'd been sewn shut. I noted with satisfaction, though, that I could hear my pulse beeping. At least I wasn't dead.

With herculean effort, I ripped the stitches from my eyelids, cracking my eyes open for the first time, I was later told, in two weeks. Dee had given me CPR and I had died twice on the way to the hospital, but they brought me back. They operated to remove the bullets, only two of which were still in me. The shoulder shot was a clean through-and-through, as was another that blew off a love handle. Two hit me center mass, though, one coming within millimeters of my heart. The surgery was apparently extremely dangerous, with the possibility of finishing the job that the bullets couldn't. They nearly lost me four more times and I had been in a coma ever since. The doctor told Dee I should be dead and that he guessed I had something too important to live for. But I knew nothing of this. For me, it was mere moments from when I was shot to when I woke up in the ICU at Northwestern Medical Center. Something tickled at the back of my mind, like I had had a dream, but I couldn't remember what it was no matter how hard I concentrated.

It took a few seconds to get my eyes to focus, but eventually I could make out three or four indistinct moving figures in the distance. I tried to raise my hand to rub my eyes but realized both my hands were tethered to the sides of the bed. One blurry blob moved closer, eventually coalescing into the most glorious sight I'd ever seen: Dee's cherubic face. She looked tired.

"Oh Harry!" There was a quake in her voice. "I thought I'd lost you." I could see tears flooding out of the corners of her eyes and pouring down her cheeks. She was immediately joined by my parents, who looked care-worn and haggard but joyous. Dee hit the call light, which was answered first by a nurse, who looked in, smiled, and shouted something I didn't understand. A few minutes later, a doctor came in, looked at me, looked at my chart, watched the machines recording my heart rate and blood pressure for a few seconds, and then looked at me with a shake of his head.

"You are one tough dude." He talked quietly with the nurse. I was beginning to get my eyes to focus better. He was a small, balding man of indeterminate Asian descent. When he came closer, I could see his name was Dr. Zerudo. The nurse, a good four inches taller than he, was only of average height, perhaps 5 feet 6 inches. Her skin was the color of chocolate with long, straight honey tinted hair that luxuriantly spilled halfway down her back in a ponytail. I thought for a second she was Beyoncé, but then I decided I was probably still a little groggy and the chances of a famous singer being my nurse were probably not that great. "Glad to have you back, Mr. Shalan." He had no discernible accent. "Would you like to have that tube out of your throat?"

I nodded as vigorously as I could, though that wasn't saying much. I'd been awake a grand total of five minutes and I already felt like taking a nap. The nurse left the room and came back a minute later with something in a plastic bag. I didn't know what it was. The doctor asked everyone to step out for a minute. My mom and dad started for the door, but Dee wouldn't budge.

"I used to be a nurse. I've seen this stuff before. I am not leaving him."

The doctor looked at me and then at Dee, and then just shrugged his shoulders. The nurse took up a position on the side of the bed opposite the doctor. She fiddled with the tube somehow. I was too tired to pay much attention. She then used suction to clear the tube and then the doctor told me to try to cough. I tried and as I did, it felt like he was pulling Ford F150 out of my throat. Eventually all 30 feet or so of the tube were out and I really was ready for a nap. The nurse put an oxygen mask over my mouth and nose and adjusted the rubber strap so it fit snugly. She could have put a pillow over my face and I wouldn't have had the energy to argue. Despite the irritation in my throat and the dryness of my mouth, all I wanted to do was sleep, but no one seemed to want to let me. The doctor and/or nurses were in and out every few minutes and Dee, God bless her, was right there at my side, talking a mile a minute. I only caught bits and pieces of it, but I did gather that Johnny and Lilith were both dead, as was Bell, which I already knew.

I would mourn Bell no more than one would mourn the loss of a cockroach after smashing it with a shoe, but I would, when sufficiently recovered, grieve deeply for the loss of two of my oldest friends and mentors. Despite the fact that, in their last, dark moments of life, both shot me, one in an attempt to kill Dee, their influence in my life was not diminished by the tragic way their lives ended. A large part of who I became as an adult had to do with the wise words and unending love of these two people. As much as I would grieve for their loss, I would grieve for how two noble lives had fallen into such darkness and ignominy. A tear escaped my eye and rolled across my cheek, nestling in my left ear. Dee looked at me, concerned.

"What's wrong Harry? Are you hurting?"

I shook my head, reaching my now untethered hand to my face, lifting up my oxygen mask. I tried twice to gather enough moisture in my mouth, but there was just none to be had. I nodded wearily to the glass on a rolling patient table at the foot of the bed. Dee looked back at where I was nodding, inferred my need and retrieved the glass. She carefully spooned a small chip of ice into my mouth. I knew how the earth must feel when the first drops of rain fall after a prolonged drought. My mouth sufficiently moistened, I drew her ear to my mouth and whispered to her in a rough croak.

"I love you baby doll."

She drew back and looked at me, fresh tears escaping her eyes. She kissed my cheek tenderly and placed her mouth gently to my ear. "I love you too, mister man."

Epilogue

Under a brilliant azure sky, the midmorning air was warm enough to drive with the Tankmobile's windows down. It was still early enough in summer that the heavily oppressive air hadn't yet set in. Dee, resplendent in a pink low-cut halter dress that was short enough to show her gorgeous gams from just above mid-thigh to her cute little feet, which were shod in dark brown ankle-length gladiator sandals that contrasted nicely with her porcelain skin and crimson toenails, was driving as I enjoyed the scenery on the Bluegrass Parkway. It had been a long recovery period for me and we were excited to get away for a real vacation. It took me quite a while to get my strength back, but the way my body was reacting to how scantily she was clad seemed a good sign.

I must have dozed off, because we were suddenly pulling into the parking lot of Bettie's Diner. Bettie was waiting for us at the door, which was no surprise at all. What we weren't expecting, though, was to see Katelyn Todd and Mike Franks sitting inside. Franks was in uniform, but Kate was in civvies because she had, we would soon learn, joined the secret service and was moving to DC in just a few days. We climbed out and both hugged Bettie before going inside. She led us to Kate and Mike's table, the exact same booth we'd been in the very first time we were there. On the way past the revolving dessert case, I searched in vain for my beloved peanut butter pie. I was crestfallen. To come all this way only to miss out on the greatest dessert—no, the greatest food of any kind—in the entire history of mankind. I was starting to wonder if all those months of recuperation had been worth it. But as I approached the table, what to my wondering eyes did appear? Not a piece of this heavenly delight, but an entire pie sat in the middle of the table, along with plates, forks, napkins, and five mugs. After hugs and handshakes, Dee slid into the nearest side of the booth with me close behind, while Bettie brought a chair from behind the bar.

"Alice," she called to the woman behind the counter, "bring us some coffee, will you, honey?"

Bettie cut the pie, giving me a full quarter and lesser pieces to everyone else. It was a religious moment. I closed my eyes and thanked God that I could live to experience this delicacy once again. After a few bites, I calmed down enough to be able to communicate with the outside world. Four sets of eyes watched me, and I realized

I probably looked like an idiot. I began laughing so hard I nearly shot peanut butter pie out of my nose. They joined in and then we fell into convivial chatter. As hard as it is to believe, I finished Kate and Dee's pieces, after which, I actually had to unbuckle my belt and pants, but I was blissful. We chatted and drank coffee for another half hour before a shadow passed over our booth, blocking out the sun.

"Well, well, well, if it ain't me old friend Harry!"

"Hagrid!" I shouted and stood to shake his mammoth hand. This wasn't good enough for this man I'd only met once but I felt I'd known forever. I guess he felt the same, because he crushed me in a hug until I saw stars.

"I heard you got yourself shot. Was afraid you'd miss out on me surprise. This is the lovely Deanna, is it? Rubeus Coltrane, I am."

Dee reached out her hand and shook his. It looked like a Barbie hand inside a regular human one.

"It's a pleasure to finally meet you. Thank you for the car."

"Speaking of cars, if you two will come with me, I can't wait any longer. If you'll kindly step outside."

HARSH PREY

I had in the back of my mind what I hoped it would be, but there was just no way it could be. There wasn't a straight piece of sheet metal on her. The trunk was crushed and the engine block had even been shot up. It was just too much to hope. Yet there she was. Ellie. She was parked next to the Tankmobile, gleaming proudly in the midday sun. It was like she'd been resurrected from the dead. I wasn't sure I could find speech I was so excited and overcome with gratitude to this giant human—giant on the inside and the outside.

"I don't even know what to say. Thank you seems so inadequate."

"No thanks needed, Harry," he said, walking up behind me and covering my entire right shoulder with the palm of his hand. "It was me great pleasure to get to work on such a lovely car as Ellie here. I find, though, that I just don't quite fit inside. I considered taking out the driver's seat, but thought it might bring down the trade-in value. Anyways, I miss me old girl. She and I just fit. Now, what say we call it an even trade?"

I started to argue, but realized it would do no good, so I just nodded and patted his hand with mine. If I wanted to keep my membership in the he-man club, I really needed to stop crying all the time. Dee handed him the keys to the Tankmobile and he traded our luggage into Ellie's trunk while she retrieved a few items from the front of the car. Finally, he handed me Ellie's key and shook my hand. As I continued around the car, I realized that she wasn't, in fact, exactly as she had been before the wreck. At the very back left corner of the hood was painted a jagged black design that looked at first like a lightning bolt, but when examining it closer and seeing the ragged edges, I realized was a scar.

"Hagrid," I said, rubbing my hand reverently across the spot, "is this?"

"Yeah." He climbed into his car and fired the engine. As he backed out, he stopped and rolled down his window.

"I'd say the man who lived deserves the car who lived."

38015254R00186

Made in the USA
Charleston, SC
26 January 2015